**Luke stepped in front of her, holding his finger to his lips again to tell her to be quiet.**

She flung her arms around his waist and gave him a tight hug before stepping back. The look of surprise on his face had her feeling foolish. But then he pulled her close and hugged her, and leaned down with his lips pressed close to her ear.

"Glad you're okay, too, but you should have stayed upstairs in the closet. Or better yet," he whispered, "you should have gotten out of here and hid in the woods."

She shook her head and pulled back. "I'm not leaving you here alone. So you'd better figure out a way to include me in your plans."

His brows lowered. "You promised."

"I know, and I'm sorry. But it wasn't a promise I should have given."

# THE
# BODYGUARD

—

## LENA DIAZ

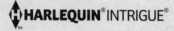

Recycling programs
for this product may
not exist in your area.

I dedicate this book to abused women everywhere.
It's not your fault. It's NEVER your fault that someone
else chooses to hurt you. You deserve a life without fear.
Please, don't wait until it's too late. For information or
help, visit The National Domestic Violence Hotline at
www.thehotline.org. (The website has a quick escape
option in case your abuser monitors your internet activity).
Or call 1-800-799-SAFE(7233) or TTY 1-800-787-3224.

ISBN-13: 978-0-373-69763-2

THE BODYGUARD

Copyright © 2014 by Lena Diaz

All rights reserved. Except for use in any review, the reproduction or
utilization of this work in whole or in part in any form by any electronic,
mechanical or other means, now known or hereafter invented, including
xerography, photocopying and recording, or in any information storage
or retrieval system, is forbidden without the written permission of the
publisher, Harlequin Enterprises Limited, 225 Duncan Mill Road,
Don Mills, Ontario M3B 3K9, Canada.

This is a work of fiction. Names, characters, places and incidents are
either the product of the author's imagination or are used fictitiously,
and any resemblance to actual persons, living or dead, business
establishments, events or locales is entirely coincidental.

This edition published by arrangement with Harlequin Books S.A.

For questions and comments about the quality of this book,
please contact us at CustomerService@Harlequin.com.

® and TM are trademarks of Harlequin Enterprises Limited or its
corporate affiliates. Trademarks indicated with ® are registered in the
United States Patent and Trademark Office, the Canadian Trade Marks
Office and in other countries.

Printed in U.S.A.

www.Harlequin.com

## ABOUT THE AUTHOR

Lena Diaz was born in Kentucky and has also lived in California, Louisiana and Florida, where she now resides with her husband and two children. Before becoming a romantic suspense author, she was a computer programmer. A former Romance Writers of America Golden Heart® finalist, she has won a prestigious Daphne du Maurier Award for excellence in mystery and suspense. She loves to watch action movies, garden and hike in the beautiful Tennessee Smoky Mountains. To get the latest news about Lena, please visit her website, www.lenadiaz.com.

## Books by Lena Diaz

HARLEQUIN INTRIGUE
1405—THE MARSHAL'S WITNESS
1422—EXPLOSIVE ATTRACTION
1466—UNDERCOVER TWIN
1476—TENNESSEE TAKEDOWN
1496—THE BODYGUARD

# CAST OF CHARACTERS

**Luke Dawson**—Bodyguard and owner of Dawson's Personal Security Services, he believes Richard Ashton's killer has a new target—Richard's widow, Caroline. Luke will do whatever it takes to help her survive and overcome the horrors of her past.

**Caroline Ashton**—After suffering emotional and physical abuse from her husband, she finally escapes, only to discover her husband's body and become embroiled in his murder investigation.

**Daniel Ashton**—Caroline's wealthy brother-in-law is polite but distant, and may know more about his brother's murder than he reveals to the police.

**Grant Ashton**—This Ashton has a hot temper and financial problems, but does that make him a killer?

**Mitch Brody**—Office manager of Dawson's Personal Security Services. He used to work for Stellar Security, one of Luke's rivals and a company Caroline doesn't trust.

**Alex Buchanan**—As a favor to his friend Luke, this semiretired defense attorney takes on Caroline as a client. But when she makes some surprising decisions, it's Alex's turn to question her role—innocent victim, or something more sinister?

**Detective Cornell**—Relentless in his pursuit of the killer, Cornell doesn't care about society's rules or being politically correct. No one gets away with murder on his watch.

**Leslie Harrison**—Caroline's only friend and confidante is also Richard Ashton's business attorney. Is she helping Caroline escape the abuse, or setting her up to take the fall?

# Chapter One

The monster sat across the breakfast table from Caroline, looking deceptively handsome in a dove-gray, thousand-dollar suit that emphasized his broad shoulders and the bulging muscles in his upper arms. The tanned hand that flicked the page on his electronic tablet was elegant, strong, with perfectly groomed nails.

They should have been talons.

Talons would have warned people who didn't know Richard Ashton III that those hands were lethal, especially when they were clasped into fists.

He skimmed through the latest stock-market figures, then looked pointedly at the untouched food on Caroline's plate.

In spite of the worry that had kept her awake most of the night, the worry that had nausea churning in her stomach this morning, she picked up her fork and took a bite of egg the cook had prepared exactly to Richard's specifications. She dabbed her napkin on the corners of her mouth as he'd taught her, before training her face into the carefully blank expression she'd learned was the safest.

His brows lowered. "You're getting too thin, Caroline. That displeases me."

She stilled, her fingers curling against her thigh.

"I—I—I'm sorry, Richard."

*Calm down. He hates it when you stutter.*

She fought back the fear that so often jumbled her words. "I'll eat everything on my plate. I promise." She took another bite of egg.

Tiny lines of disapproval tightened around his eyes.

Her stomach twisted. What had she done? She raced through a mental checklist. Her hair was neat and curled to drape over one shoulder in the style he preferred. She'd painstakingly applied the makeup he'd selected for her, natural looking but polished. She held her napkin in her left hand in her lap, her fork in her right, no elbows on the table. What had she missed?

"Don't look so alarmed," he chided her. He cocked his head, his eyes narrowing. "Or have you done something that requires further instruction?"

"No, no, no, I've been good. I don't…n-need another l-lesson."

*Stop it. Calm down.*

"Don't stutter, Caroline. It's unbecoming of an Ashton to stutter. Tell me, why aren't you eating enough?"

Her hands went clammy with sweat and shook so badly she almost dropped her fork. Desperation had her scooping another forkful of eggs into her mouth. As she chewed, she smiled across the table at him, trying to placate him.

He shook his head. "You're being rude. I asked you a question, and now your mouth is full. You're making me wait for an answer."

*Stupid, stupid, stupid.* She should have answered him first and then taken a bite. She swallowed hard, forcing the lump of eggs down her tight throat without taking the time to chew.

"I'm so sorry," she rushed to assure him. "I didn't

mean to be rude. I w-wanted you to be proud that I was obeying, that I was eating." She wiped her moist hands on her pants.

"I'm still waiting for an answer."

She blinked. What was the question? What *was* it? She couldn't remember. He'd said something about her being too thin, and then he'd said—

"I asked why you aren't eating enough." His voice was clipped, harsh.

"I'm s-sorry. I guess I'm just…tired. Not hungry."

One of his elegant brows arched. "And why, *exactly,* are you tired?"

She grasped for an excuse, anything but the truth— that she'd lain awake most of the night, going over her plans, trying to build her courage.

"I—I don't know. Perhaps I worked too hard in the garden yesterday. I *am* a bit sore."

The slight reddening of his face had the blood draining from hers, leaving her cold and full of dread. He would take her comment about being sore as an accusation against him, a complaint. Because, as he frequently reminded her, it was always *her* fault when he was forced to teach her a lesson, *her* fault he had to punish her.

"You've worked in the garden plenty of times without being sore." His voice lashed out at her like a whip. "I'm more inclined to believe you're complaining that you forced me to teach you a lesson yesterday."

She dropped her gaze, her pulse slamming in her ears. A whimper bubbled up inside her, but she couldn't let it escape. Crying was undignified. Ashtons did *not* cry.

"Look at me when I'm speaking to you," he demanded.

"Please," she whispered, trying to appeal to the man he *used* to be, the man that must surely still be there, somewhere, hidden deep inside, the man she'd loved once, so very long ago. "Please, Richard. It was a...poor choice of words. I'm sorry."

He plopped his napkin on the table and stood. "Yes, it certainly was, a very poor choice." He stalked to her chair.

She shrank back and hated herself for it.

The cook walked into the dining room, smiling a greeting at Richard, ignoring Caroline, as she'd been ordered to do. As they'd *all* been ordered to do. The staff knew Richard was the perfect, loving husband saddled with an unbalanced wife who made his life miserable—a wife who was to be ignored, for her own safety, lest she get too worked up. A wife who must never be allowed to leave the estate without her husband, except for her once-a-week errands, which were carefully timed and reported upon so Richard could immediately come to her aid if she became confused. Only Richard knew how to handle her, how to take care of her, how to keep her calm, or so they all believed.

At times like this, Caroline almost believed the lies herself. After all, she had to be insane to have stayed with the devil as long as she had.

"Mr. Ashton, good morning to you. Can I get you anything else, sir?" the cook asked.

His face smoothed out and he returned her smile. "Yes. Please let Charles know I'll be leaving a bit later than planned." He circled his fingers around Caroline's wrists and pulled her to her feet, smiling the entire time. "Have him bring the car around front in exactly one hour. Mrs. Ashton and I would like to...talk."

He added a wink that had the cook blushing and assuming exactly what he wanted her to assume—that he was a loving husband intent on loving his wife.

"Very good, sir." She hurried out of the room.

Richard's grip on Caroline's wrists turned crushingly brutal.

She gasped and tried to pull her hands back. "Please, you're hurting me."

He immediately let go, frowning at the red marks he'd left. "Later, you will change into long sleeves. I won't have someone misinterpreting anything they might see. Now, come along. Apparently yesterday's lesson was insufficient."

He put his hand on the small of her back. She tottered on shaking legs toward the winding marble staircase in the two-story foyer.

She could endure this. She could get through this. She could survive this.

Those three sentences went through her mind over and over, like a prayer, giving her the strength to climb the stairs with her husband at her side, towering over her, like a prison guard leading an inmate to the death chamber.

At the first landing, he caught her shoulders, turned her around and kissed her. She was so stunned she forgot to pretend to respond. He broke the kiss and pressed his lips close to her ear.

"Close your eyes, Caroline. Kiss me back."

She saw the reason then for his pretend affection. A maid had entered the foyer below. This was part of Richard's game, making others believe he was devoted to her. Appearances were everything to an Ashton.

His lips touched hers again. When the hard ridge of his erection pressed against her belly, she shuddered with revulsion. His arms tightened painfully around her bruised side where he'd kicked her last night. She fervently hoped he'd taken her shudder for passion instead of disgust, or her lesson would be more severe than usual.

He led her to the master bedroom at the end of the hall.

As he closed the thick, soundproof double doors behind them, she reminded herself again that she'd endured his lessons many times. She could survive one more. She had to. Because after today, she would be free. After today, she would never see Richard Ashton III again.

He yanked her long hair, jerking her backward, twisting her neck at an impossible angle. She sucked in a sharp breath, loathing and despair boiling up inside her. His eyes darkened with the anticipation she'd grown to dread, even as he shook his head like a teacher bitterly disappointed with his star pupil.

She knew what he would say next, the same thing he said every time he "instructed" her, the same thing he would tell her when he plunged into her bruised and battered body to slake the lust that always consumed him after giving her a lesson.

"I love you, Caroline. I do this *because* I love you." The disappointment in his voice might have been convincing if it weren't for the anticipation that had his mouth curving into a feral smile.

His eyes narrowed when she didn't rush to say what she was supposed to say.

Perhaps it was the knowledge that this was the last time she'd ever have to endure his touch that made her brave. She glared at him, refusing to give him the words he wanted.

He grabbed her upper arms, his fingers digging into her with bruising force.

The pressure made her cry out. Unwelcome tears pricked the backs of her eyes. "Please, stop."

"Say it!" His fingers dug harder, like the talons she'd pictured earlier.

Her vision blurred.

"I love you," she choked out, despising him all the

more for the coward he'd forced her to become. But she would say the empty, meaningless words a thousand times if it would stop the blinding pain. "I love you, I love you, I love—"

"And?" He shook her, snapping her teeth together, making her bite the inside of her cheek. The metallic taste of blood filled her mouth.

"I—I'm…s-sorry."

He abruptly let her go. She staggered back. A wave of dizziness sent her wobbling to the nearest piece of furniture in the expansive room, the four-poster bed. She clung to one of the thick posts. The pain that lanced through her upper arms made her cry out again.

His nostrils flared. He stalked toward her, shedding his clothes as he approached, his arousal stiff and heavy, an unyielding sword to wield against her. She cringed against the bed as the monster's perfect hand coiled into a fist.

## Chapter Two

Another wave of nausea hit Caroline. She clutched the edge of the receptionist's desk and drew in deep breaths, fighting the dizziness that had plagued her since she'd dragged her aching body out of bed this morning. Richard's "lesson" yesterday had delayed her plans by a full day. But nothing would stop her this time. She'd just have to fight through the pain.

"Mrs. Ashton, are you okay?" The receptionist hurried around the desk, her youthful face mirroring concern.

"She's fine." Leslie Harrison, the Harrison part of the law firm of Wiley & Harrison, admonished the other woman. "I'll escort Mrs. Ashton to her car."

"Yes, ma'am." The receptionist resumed her seat, aiming a resentful look at her boss's back.

"Leslie, I'm actually not feeling all that well. Perhaps I should sit down for a moment."

"Come along, Caroline. You'll feel better when you get out of this stuffy office into the fresh air." She leaned in close. "It's just nerves." Her voice was low so no one else would hear her as she escorted Caroline outside the busy lobby. "You're taking a huge step today. Besides, you don't have a minute to waste if you're going to get to the new house before your husband discovers you're missing."

Caroline gave her a shaky smile. "I'm sorry. You've gone to a lot of trouble to help me. I don't mean to sound ungrateful." She clicked her key fob and unlocked the black Mercedes S600 sedan Richard had chosen for her. Not for the first time, she wished he would allow her to drive something simpler, less pretentious.

Leslie held the car door open. "No worries, dear. I'm happy to help. Remember, go straight to the new house. No stops along the way. Promise me."

"I promise."

Leslie smiled and stepped back as Caroline eased into the driver's seat.

A few miles down the road, another wave of dizziness hit. A sharp cramp shot through her belly. She yanked the wheel, pulling to the shoulder of the road amid a flurry of honking horns as other drivers swerved to avoid her.

Sweat popped out on her forehead in spite of the cold air blasting out of the air-conditioning vents. She tried to sit as still as she could, willing the dizziness and pain away. Being sore the morning after one of Richard's lessons wasn't unusual. But for some reason it was so much worse today. It must be nerves, as Leslie had said. She'd been plotting her escape for months. And now that she was actually going through with her plan, the stress was making her sick.

She worried her bottom lip with her teeth and clutched her cramping belly. Richard's extra lesson had almost ruined everything, making it physically impossible for her to do her Wednesday chores. But this morning it was Richard who insisted that she couldn't be lazy two days in a row. He'd ordered her to get out of bed to take care of the errands she'd skipped yesterday. Her eagerness to do his bidding had pleased him. What he didn't realize was that he'd given her a gift by ordering her to go.

After breakfast she'd stood at the door and waved goodbye to her husband for the last time while Charles pulled the Rolls-Royce around the circular driveway. Richard closely watched her through the rolled-down window in the backseat. His suspicious gaze had her clutching the doorway, worried she'd done something to give away her plans. But the car hadn't stopped, and Richard continued down the road toward his office.

Careful not to do anything that might trigger a call from the household staff to her husband, she'd stuck to her usual weekly itinerary of going to the dry cleaner's and then to the lawyer's office. The difference this time was that instead of dropping off her clothes with Richard's at the cleaner's, she'd only dropped off Richard's. She kept the small bag of her clothes and toiletries she'd carefully packed to begin her new life. Using the dry-cleaning trip as her excuse, she'd been able to carry her bag out of the house without tipping off the security guards that something was different.

After the cleaner's, she drove to the lawyer's office to deliver the accordion of tax receipts and documents to Leslie and to supposedly collect any papers Richard needed to review or sign. Of course, this week, there would be no return trip to give him anything. She wasn't going back.

Since he could have ordered any number of people to perform both chores every week, Caroline assumed her errands were some kind of test. So she'd always been careful to go straight to the cleaner's, then straight to the lawyer, then straight home.

The clock in the dashboard had her hands tightening on the steering wheel. Leslie had warned her not to make any stops. She didn't have time to sit on the side of the highway, no matter how much she hurt. In exactly twelve minutes, the security detail would notify her husband she wasn't home. Richard would call Leslie and ask when Caroline had left. Once he realized she hadn't gone straight home, he'd leave the office and go searching for her.

She lifted a shaky hand to her brow. Dear Lord, what was she doing? What had made her think she could escape? She debated turning around and racing back home. But even if she managed not to get pulled over for speeding, she'd never make it in time. How would she explain being late?

If she told the truth, that she'd been sick and had pulled over, he probably wouldn't believe her. But even if he did, he'd accuse her of complaining again. It was her fault that she felt bad, and she shouldn't make him worry or have to come check on her just because she couldn't accept the consequences of her actions. He'd feel compelled to "instruct" her again.

She clenched her teeth. She was already one huge mass of bruises. Everything hurt. Endure another lesson? No, she couldn't, she just *couldn't*.

Protection. She needed protection. But who could protect her? She had no friends, no family—not in Savannah, anyway. And her parents wouldn't exactly be pleased to find out she'd left her wealthy husband. They'd be worried the monthly checks Richard sent them would stop.

Who else, then? Leslie was the only person she ever dared to speak to outside the house, unless she was with her husband at some function. And since her duty at those functions was to cling to his arm like a decoration and not leave his side, she never had the opportunity to foster any friendships.

But she couldn't ask Leslie to outright defy Richard by harboring her. Leslie's law practice depended on Ashton Enterprises' lucrative account. Jeopardizing Leslie's income wasn't fair, especially after everything the lawyer had already done to help her. No, she'd started down this path. She had to see it through. So, what, then? What *could* she do?

The idea of going to the police flitted through her mind but was quickly discarded. She'd seen the shows on TV. The cops couldn't do much until *after* a crime was committed, except maybe tell her to get a restraining order. And what was the use of a flimsy piece of paper against a man as rich and powerful as Richard Ashton III?

Not that a judge would believe her and give her a restraining order in the first place. Society worshipped and adored Richard. To them, he was a generous humanitarian who donated millions every year to charity and supported the campaigns of just about everyone holding office in Savannah right now, including the sheriff of Chatham County. No, going to the police wasn't an option.

Then how could she protect herself? Richard's idea of protection was a twenty-four-hour guard at the house. Maybe that was what she needed: her own guard, someone who would be loyal to *her* and only her.

She drew her hand across her damp brow and used her car's voice-command center to search the phone book for "bodyguards in Savannah, Georgia." She selected the first company that popped up in the search results and set the GPS to direct her there.

IF HER ROYAL HIGHNESS—Kate Middleton—had materialized in the offices of Dawson's Personal Security Services, it would have surprised Luke Dawson far less than the woman who'd just stepped through his door: Caroline

Ashton—beautiful, platinum blonde, wife of billionaire businessman Richard Ashton III.

Luke couldn't say what designers had made her tasteful silky tan skirt and matching blazer, or the tiny, shimmering handbag hanging off her shoulder. But he did know her clothes were expensive—and totally out of place in the cramped, dusty office that normally catered to hookers looking for protection from their pimps, or small-business owners needing protection when they got behind with their bookies.

Obviously, she was lost.

He glanced at the only other person in the room, his office manager, Mitch Brody, sitting a few feet away. Mitch shrugged, indicating he didn't know what was going on, either.

Luke waited for their guest to say something, but she simply stood in front of his desk as if she was waiting for permission to speak—probably some quirk of the superrich. He shoved his chair back and offered his hand to shake.

"I'm Luke Dawson. And that's Mitch Brody. What can Dawson's Personal Security Services do for you, Mrs. Ashton?"

Her blue eyes widened, providing a stark contrast to her pale complexion. Was she surprised he knew her name? Didn't she realize *everyone* in Savannah knew who the Ashtons were? The "perfect couple" was plastered on the front pages of the local gossip rags at least once a week, and their annual Christmas party was the event of the social season, rivaling the acclaim of the infamous parties held by Jim Williams back in his heyday. Or at least, that was what Luke had *heard.* His name would certainly never appear on the Ashtons' Christmas party's prestigious guest list.

She swayed slightly, as if caught in a daydream, before stretching her manicured hand out to shake his.

His hand practically swallowed hers, and he felt a shudder go through her. What the hell? She pulled her hand back, but not before he noticed something flash in her eyes, something he'd seen too many times in his line of work not to recognize it.

*Fear.*

Was it possible she was here on purpose, and that she needed help? That seemed so unlikely as to sound ludicrous, but Luke's internal radar sounded a warning. Rather than show her to the door as he'd been tempted to do the moment she'd walked in, he rounded his desk and picked up a stack of folders from the one guest chair he owned.

He frowned at the lint on the dark green fabric. Normally he wouldn't give it a second thought, but Caroline Ashton was far too sophisticated to sit on a dirty chair.

"Give me a minute and I'll find something to cover the seat."

"No, no, please. Don't go to any trouble on my behalf. This is fine."

She sat before he could stop her.

He raised a brow in surprise and leaned back against the edge of the desk, his legs stretched out in front of him as he waited for her to explain why she was here. But again, she seemed perfectly content not to say anything. She simply looked up at him with a polite, blank look. He wondered again at the foibles of the wealthy.

"Mrs. Ashton, how can we help you today?"

"I n-need t-to…" She squeezed her eyes shut for a moment as if she was in pain. "I need to hire a bodyguard."

Her nervousness had him studying her more closely.

"I figured you came in here by accident and needed directions."

Her thick lashes dipped down to her lap, as if keeping eye contact was too difficult.

"I'm not lost. I need protection."

Her words, and the desperate quality of her voice, had those alarms ringing in his head like church bells on Sunday. Still, he didn't want to offend her if he'd misunderstood—because surely a billionaire's wife didn't really need Luke's protection.

"Mrs. Ashton, it's no secret that your husband has a contract with Stellar Security, one of the best security firms in Georgia, one of my biggest competitors." He glanced at Mitch, who'd gone stone-faced as soon as Luke mentioned Mitch's former employer. Mitch hated Stellar Security, but since he'd never explained why, Luke could only go by his own personal dealings with the other firm.

"I wish I could tell you my company could do better," he continued, "but honestly, I don't have the resources the other firm has. I have five bodyguards, besides myself. Stellar has dozens. If someone's bothering you, I can call your husband's security guys and talk to them for you."

She shook her head, her eyes widening. "No, don't call them. They're the last people I would trust."

He frowned. "Why wouldn't you trust them? They work for you."

For the first time since coming into the office, she seemed to really focus on him. The blank look evaporated, replaced by a look of startling clarity and intelligence, as if she'd been playing a role earlier and she'd decided to drop all pretenses.

"No. They *don't* work for me. They work for my husband."

Few people surprised Luke Dawson anymore, but

Caroline Ashton had just given him a sucker punch. Was it possible she was afraid of her *husband?* If something… bad…was going on between them, Luke would have expected rumors in those gossip magazines. At the very least, he'd expect to hear something in the bars when he and his security friends bantered about their clients and the crazy things they sometimes did. But he'd never heard a whisper of anything bad about the Ashton couple. Not one.

He *had* heard the exact opposite, that Richard Ashton III was practically a saint, in spite of his wife being a bit…needy, to put it kindly. She was said to be nervous, high-strung, but her husband was the epitome of tenderness whenever they were seen together. He was always at her side, seeing to her every whim.

Luke studied her face. Her skin tone was even, her makeup accenting her natural beauty, not thick like women wore when trying to cover bruises. Long sleeves covered her arms—no clues there. But her legs, at least what he could see beneath her modest, below-the-knee skirt, were long and sleek, without the hint of a bump or a bruise. There was *nothing* about her appearance that made him think she had valid reasons to fear her husband.

With everything he'd heard about the Ashtons, he *should* believe she'd come here, like so many women before her, planning a divorce and hoping to use the "abuse excuse" to take her husband for everything he was worth. That would make sense, except for one thing.

*The fear in her eyes is real.* He'd bet his autographed Tom Glavine baseball on it.

Still, just in case he was wrong, he proceeded as he would with any other client, probing for the facts.

"Let me guess. You're getting a divorce, and you want a bodyguard until the divorce is final."

Her eyes widened again. "I haven't filed yet, but that's my intention, yes. I've rented a house outside of town. I'm on my way there now. I just need someone to stay with me until things are…settled."

That admission sent a flash of disappointment through him. Maybe he was wrong about the fear in her eyes. Maybe she *was* just like those other women, the ones who would tarnish their husbands' reputations with ugly lies so they could profit financially when their relationships went south.

"You need a bodyguard right now?"

"Yes."

He straightened away from the desk. Regardless of the kind of person she was, he couldn't afford to turn away a paying client. He had too many unpaying ones to allow that luxury and keep his business afloat.

As for going on assignment right now, that wasn't a problem. He kept a go-bag packed at all times with his clothes and extra ammunition. Since Luke needed to keep his hands free while guarding a client, Mitch would load the bag into the car while Luke escorted the client outside. Standard operating procedure, and so routine he didn't even need to remind Mitch, who had already jumped out of his chair and grabbed the go-bag. He stood waiting beside Luke's desk with the strap over his shoulder.

"We can leave right after you sign a contract and pay a retainer fee," Luke said. "Do you want to take your car or mine?"

Her cheeks flushed a light pink. "Mr. Dawson, I mean no disrespect, but you're a bit…small. Is there someone else you could assign to help me?"

He stared at her in stunned amazement. Mitch shook his head, obviously as confused as Luke was.

Luke crossed his arms over his chest. "Mrs. Ashton, in all my thirty years, no one else has ever called me small. I'm six foot three and weigh two hundred twenty pounds. I'm not bragging when I say most of that is muscle. It's just a fact, a necessity of my occupation. I was a champion boxer in high school and college. I'm extensively trained in self-defense. I carry a concealed weapon, am a crack shot and I know just about everything there is to know about guarding people. I assure you, I'm more than capable of protecting you."

She politely cleared her throat, not looking all that impressed with his speech. "Have you ever met my husband?"

"Not in person, no. But I've seen pictures of him." He leaned back against the desk again and braced his hands on the edge while he waited for her explanation.

"Richard is a very…large, strong, determined man. He can be…dangerous. He's extremely… If he were to… I just…" She let out a deep sigh. "I need to know that you would be safe if…*when*…he comes looking for me."

This time, there could be no doubt that the fear in her voice, in her expression, was real. It was palpable, a living, breathing thing, constricting around her, ready to choke her into submission.

She twisted her fingers together. The diamond ring glittering on her left hand sparkled beneath the fluorescent lights. The center stone had to be four carats, easy. It could have paid the rent on Luke's office *and* his house for a full year, with money left over.

But that wasn't why he decided he had to convince her to hire him.

He had to convince her to hire him because whether

the threat against her was real or imagined, she *believed* it was real. But even more important than that, he'd never met any clients before who were more concerned about their bodyguard's welfare than their own. A person like that deserved his protection, because he was one of the best. And regardless of who she was, she deserved something he sensed she hadn't had in a long time: someone who would look after her, someone to take her seriously, someone who would be her ally.

He waited until her haunted gaze lifted to his before answering.

"Mrs. Ashton, your husband may be a tad taller than me, possibly even brawnier. But fighting isn't all about size. It's about training, experience, strategy. I don't have the slightest doubt I can handle him in a fight…if it comes to that. The best strategy is to avoid a fight if at all possible. But if you hire me, I'll guard you with my life. I will do everything I can to keep you safe. And I'll make sure your husband never gets anywhere near you again. That's a promise. And I never, *ever* break a promise."

Unshed tears brightened her eyes, inexplicably making Luke want to pull her close and hold her until the fear subsided and the shadows in her eyes disappeared.

"Thank you," she whispered, her voice shaking with obvious relief, her throat working as if she was struggling not to cry. "Thank you so much."

# Chapter Three

Caroline sat in her car in the circular driveway of the blue-and-white one-story cottage. She'd lived in a mansion for over five years. Before that, she'd lived with her parents about three hours from Savannah in the same house since the day she was born. But this plain, simple structure already felt like the home she'd never really had.

Because she wouldn't be sharing it with Richard.

A tap on her car window made her start. But it wasn't her husband's angry visage glaring at her through the glass. It was the concerned face of Luke Dawson, who'd hopped out of the car as soon as she'd parked. She'd apparently zoned out, lost in her memories, and her fears, and forgot about him. She pressed the button and lowered the window.

"Mrs. Ashton, we need to get inside. You're sitting out in the open here."

"Of course. I'm sorry. Should I pop the trunk for our luggage?"

"No…I'll get our bags after you're safely inside the house."

She rolled the window up and opened the door.

He reached for her hand. She hesitated, bracing herself not to jerk away when his much larger hand closed around hers. But when he touched her, to her surprise and relief, she didn't feel nausea or dread. Unlike her husband's touch, the warmth and strength in Luke's hand made her feel something she hadn't felt in years…safe.

She smiled up at him, but he was too busy scanning the yard and street out front to notice. As she stood, another sharp pain shot through her belly, making her wince. She was glad Luke hadn't seen that. It had been difficult enough to admit to a stranger that she was afraid of her own husband. It would be beyond humiliating for Luke to even suspect the extent of her cowardice over the years, to learn just how much she'd endured, all because she'd been too weak to stand up for herself.

A warm breeze filtered through the trees overhead, stirring his lightweight leather jacket. She'd wondered why he wore a jacket in the summer, but now she knew: to conceal the gun holstered on the hip pocket of his jeans. She'd never been this close to a gun before and had always assumed it would terrify her. But the sight of his weapon was actually reassuring. Richard might laugh at her puny attempts to deflect his blows, but even her husband wasn't immune to the ravages of a well-aimed bullet.

Luke stayed at her back as she walked the short distance to the front stoop, but as soon as she unlocked the door, he rushed her into the foyer and flipped the dead bolt behind them.

His mouth tightened into a thin line. "No security alarm?"

"Not yet. I only rented the house a little over a week ago." She rubbed her hands up and down her arms. "We've never had one at the mansion. Richard didn't like the inconvenience of having to worry about using a keypad if he decided to step outside at night."

"You didn't need one at the mansion because the estate

was gated and had security guards watching it 24/7. I'll get someone out here today to install one."

He gently pushed her aside as he opened the hall-closet door, apparently searching for intruders. Next, he glanced through the archway to their right into the family room, then back down the hallway to their left. "Stay here while I check the bedrooms."

He disappeared down the short hall. It took him less than a minute to search the two bedrooms and bath. Then he was back at her side in the foyer.

"I assume the kitchen is through the family room?" he asked.

"Yes, through that other archway." She didn't bother to add that this was her first time seeing the house in person. Leslie had handled everything for her: helping her find the house, arranging for the lease, getting the key. Caroline had only seen the house online and knew the layout from the virtual tour. There was never a chance for her to physically go to the house. Richard would never have let her out of his sight long enough for that.

Luke headed into the family room, which had a panoramic view of both the street out front and the fenced backyard. The long, narrow style of the house was one of the primary reasons Caroline had chosen it. When Richard eventually discovered where she was—and she didn't doubt that he would—she wanted to see him coming. And with both front- and rear-facing windows in most of the rooms, she'd always have an exit nearby so she could flee if she had to.

After looking behind the couch and the few other places big enough to hide someone, Luke continued into the kitchen.

A moment later, the sound of his deep voice carried to Caroline, in a one-sided conversation she couldn't quite make out. He must be talking to someone on the phone. Obviously there wasn't anything to worry about if he could take the time for that.

She wiped her brow, surprised to find it damp with perspiration. The inside of the house was nice and cool, both from the air conditioner and because of the majestic, Spanish moss–dripping oak trees that hung over the roof, shading it from the merciless summer sun.

Maybe she was catching a cold, or the flu. That would explain why she was achy all over, even in places where Richard hadn't hit her. She dropped her purse on one of the end tables that had come with the furnished cottage and headed toward the kitchen. When she stepped into the entryway, she froze.

On the far side of the room, Luke was talking to someone on his cell phone. But on the white tile floor at his feet, lying in a pool of blood, was Richard Ashton III.

The room began to spin. Richard had found her already. How? It was a trick. It had to be. Any second now he would jump up and point an accusing finger at her. Then he'd teach her another lesson. Her eyes widened as she stared at him. The blood. *No, no, no.* The blood was soaking into his favorite Italian suit—the suit he'd worn the day they met. He'd *kill* her if that suit was ruined.

She took a step toward him, then stopped. She started shaking. Someone called her name. Her world tilted. Everything went black.

LUKE SHOT AN aggravated glance at the balding Chatham County police officer sitting across from him in the E.R. waiting room. "I've already told you all this, Detective Cornell."

"Then tell me again. You said you've never met Mrs. Ashton before today?"

"That's right."

"What time did she arrive at your office?"

"About 9:10."

Cornell wrote something on the old-fashioned little spiral notebook he carried. "And she was in your office how long?"

"Ten minutes, give or take. She wanted to hire a bodyguard. She signed a boilerplate contract, gave me a retainer—"

"How much?"

"How much what?"

"How much was the retainer?"

Luke shook his head. He was never big on patience anyway, but answering the detective's relentless questions had destroyed what little patience he had.

"My standard fee for a full-time assignment, two thousand a week, plus expenses."

The detective whistled. "Sounds steep."

"You get what you pay for. Look, I want to check on Mrs. Ashton."

"There's no point in checking with the nurse again. Once a doctor has time to examine her, we'll be updated about why she fainted."

Luke laughed without humor. "She didn't just 'faint.' There's something wrong with her. I couldn't wake her up. And there were bruises on her wrists, bruises that looked like handprints. Do you know how hard someone would have to squeeze a woman's wrist to leave marks like that?"

"You think her husband hurt her?"

"Don't you?"

He shrugged. "You think she was justified in killing her husband?"

Luke stilled. "You don't seriously think she's the one who killed him."

"She's the wife. She's the first person I'll look at."

"Richard Ashton was already dead when we arrived at the house. And if she's the one who killed him, why would she hire a bodyguard?"

Detective Cornell slid his notepad and pen into his shirt pocket and sank back against the unyielding hard plastic chair as if it was the most comfortable of recliners. "Sounds like a good defense, something that might give the jurors reasonable doubt. Pretty smart, if you ask me."

"Do you know the time of death yet to see if she has an alibi?"

"No. And that's the main reason I haven't arrested her."

"That, and the fact that she's unconscious, I suppose." He couldn't help the sarcasm that crept into his tone.

Cornell smiled as if amused by Luke's statement. "Yep. There's that, too."

Luke stared at the exasperating police officer. Part of him thought the detective was latching on to the easiest explanation, but another part of him agreed with Cornell. If Caroline Ashton was abused, as Luke believed, she might have planned her revenge. She may have used Luke and his company as part of that plan so someone would be with her when she "discovered" her husband's body.

That possibility didn't sit well with him. But he'd signed a contract, and he'd given her his promise. He was duty-bound to protect her until the contract expired this time next week, or until she released him from that promise.

"There's another angle to consider," Luke said. "The killer's target may have been *Mrs.* Ashton. After all, it was her house. The killer could have been waiting there for her, but the husband showed up. The killer may have felt cornered, so he shot Mr. Ashton and ran off."

The detective pursed his mouth. "I won't dismiss that out of hand. But it's not high on my list of probable scenarios."

It wasn't high on Luke's, either, but he was trying to keep more of an open mind than the jaded policeman across from him.

"I've got to make a call." Luke shoved out of the hard, narrow chair he'd stuffed his body into for over two hours while waiting for a doctor to see Caroline Ashton.

He hurried outside the waiting area and turned his cell phone on. When Mitch answered his call, Luke didn't waste time on small talk. "Have you found out anything?"

"Sure did. I called a buddy of mine who works for Stellar Security. He said they keep a log of everyone going in and out of the Ashton mansion, right down to the minute. And Mr. Ashton keeps a GPS tracker on his wife's car. Can you believe that? I have a printout of every place she went this morning, with the exact times."

A GPS tracker sounded invasive, controlling, which made Luke's suspicions about abuse even stronger. Wouldn't it be ironic if Richard Ashton's attempt to keep a tether on his wife ended up proving her innocence? "Go ahead. Tell me."

"Mr. Ashton left the house at 7:55. His wife left fifteen minutes later. She drove directly to a dry-cleaning company and stayed there for ten minutes. After that, she drove across town to Wiley & Harrison, again without making any stops along the way, arriving at precisely 8:40."

"Wiley & Harrison, the law firm?"

"One and the same. Her visit at the law office lasted

twelve minutes. After that, she headed down Highway 80, pulled over and stopped for fourteen additional minutes."

"Any clue why?"

"You'll have to ask her that."

"Okay, then what."

"You know the rest. She drove straight to our office, arriving at 9:12, hired us, and you followed her to the cottage, arriving at 9:47. You placed the 911 call four minutes later."

Luke considered what Mitch had said. "I haven't been told an official time of death yet, but Richard Ashton's body was still warm when I checked for a pulse. From what you just told me, there's no way she had the opportunity to kill him."

"Doesn't look like it."

Some of the tension went out of him. It was only then that he realized how much he'd hoped Caroline Ashton was innocent. He was normally an excellent judge of character, a skill that helped immensely in his line of work. From the beginning, Caroline had seemed kind and caring, as evidenced by her concern about whether he might get hurt protecting her. She didn't strike him as the type of woman who could murder someone, even if they deserved it.

"Thanks, Mitch."

"You bet. You need me to follow up on anything else?"

"Not right now. Just keep the office going. I'll call you later."

He headed back into the waiting room. When he updated the detective about what he'd found out, disappointment flashed across the policeman's face.

As if noticing Luke's puzzlement, Cornell gave him a lopsided smile. "I'd hoped for a quick open-and-shut case. The coroner called while you were outside. He said the victim was killed within an hour of when the body was discovered. I already confirmed Mr. Ashton arrived at his office at 8:30 and left again at 8:45. His limo driver said he dropped Mr. Ashton off at the cottage, per his instructions, twenty minutes later. That would have been about the same time Mrs. Ashton arrived at your office. If everything you just told me checks out, she didn't have the opportunity to shoot her husband."

"His limo driver dropped him off? And left him there?"

"Apparently. I've got another detective interviewing the driver right now to find out more. I'm also sending someone over to your place of business to take a statement from this Mitch guy, the one you said can vouch that Mrs. Ashton was there this morning."

"Mr. Dawson?" a voice called out. "Detective Cornell?" A doctor stood in the entrance to the waiting room, looking around at the various groups of people. Luke and Cornell both rose. The doctor hurried to them and introduced himself.

"Is Mrs. Ashton okay?" Luke asked.

"I'm hopeful for a good outcome. She's in recovery now."

"'Hopeful'?" Luke said. "'Recovery'? You had to operate?"

"She was bleeding internally, from a ruptured spleen. If she hadn't gotten here when she did, she might not have made it."

"Do you know how she was injured?" Cornell asked.

Luke shook his head. The answer was as obvious as the bruises on Caroline's wrists.

The doctor's jaw tightened. "I've got a pretty good idea. Follow me."

He led them through the double doors and turned left

down a brightly lit hall, stopping at a door marked Recovery. Inside, he brought them down a row of curtained-off enclosures to the last one at the end. He pulled the green curtain back to reveal Caroline Ashton, asleep, looking pale, vulnerable, her small body lost in the middle of the hospital bed. An IV tube ran from the back of her right hand to a bag suspended on a pole. A blood-pressure cuff was wrapped around her other arm. The monitor behind the bed beeped and displayed numbers and graphs as it tracked her vital signs.

The doctor waved to the bruises on her wrists.

For once, the detective wasn't smiling. He hadn't seen the bruises earlier, as Luke had. The sight of them now had his mouth pressing into a hard, thin line.

"I won't disturb her to show you the other bruises," the doctor said, keeping his voice low. "But I can tell you, there are plenty of them, across her abdomen, her back, her side, in places typically covered by clothing. Unless she was in several violent car wrecks recently, there's only one obvious explanation. Someone beat her, viciously, repeatedly, over a period of several days, based on the coloration of the bruises. But that's not half the story."

He crossed the small space to a computer monitor on a rolling cart. After typing a few commands, he turned the screen around to reveal an X-ray.

"This," he said, pointing to the screen, "is a healed hairline fracture on her right forearm. It was probably broken a few years ago." He punched another button to reveal a new picture. "And this is another fracture, on her other forearm. Again, it's healed, a relatively old injury, probably within the past eight or nine months." He turned the monitor back around. "I could show you more scans, but they all show the same thing—a history of injuries. None of them were compound fractures, meaning they weren't bad enough breaks to cause lasting damage or require setting. Which is probably why whoever did this to her was never forced to take her to a hospital. But those injuries should have been stabilized with a cast to aid in healing and to reduce her pain."

Luke flinched and looked down at the bed. How could someone do that to another person? Especially a woman. And especially a woman as small and delicate as this one.

"How do you know no one took her to a hospital?" Cornell asked.

"Because as soon as I saw the scans, I had my assistant call the Ashton house and talk to the staff. None of them were aware of any trips to the hospital and never saw her in a cast. We also verified that none of the hospitals in Savannah ever listed Mrs. Ashton as a patient. Either she wasn't treated for these injuries at all, or she was treated out of town, or possibly seen in a private office by a doctor who didn't know her history of other injuries. If a doctor only saw her once, for one fracture, he might not have had any reason to suspect domestic violence. But this last time, her abuser went too far, ruptured her spleen, nearly killed her. But that's still not the worst of it."

Luke's head whipped up. "What could possibly be worse?"

"Mrs. Ashton is septic. She's on IV antibiotics and will be moved from Recovery to Intensive Care soon."

"Why is she septic?" Luke asked.

"Because she was recently pregnant. I suspect she lost the baby during a beating, and she never had medical treatment. I performed a D & C to scrape out her uterus. If she's lucky, she'll respond to the antibiotics."

"And if she isn't lucky?" Cornell asked, his notebook out again.

"She could die."

A nurse came into the room and whispered something to the doctor.

"I have to check on another patient, gentlemen," the doctor said. "I'll be back in a few minutes."

After the doctor left, Cornell flipped his notebook closed.

"I'm keeping Mrs. Ashton at the top of my persons-of-interest list."

Luke stared at him incredulously. "After what the doctor just said? You'd pursue her as a suspect?"

"Regardless of what her husband did to her, she didn't have the right to kill him. She should have reported the abuse."

"It's not that easy and you know it. I've seen enough domestic-violence cases to know people feel trapped, with nowhere to turn. Or they kid themselves into thinking the abuser is sorry, that he'll change his ways. Or worse, they blame themselves. Getting out isn't as easy as you would think from the outside looking in."

"Regardless, she's a billionaire's wife," Cornell said. "She wasn't exactly hurting for money. She could have left him. She *did* leave him. She wasn't trapped."

Luke ground his teeth together and reached for Caroline's hand. Her skin was burning up, pale, almost translucent. He couldn't begin to imagine the pain she'd suffered. Did she even know she was pregnant? Did she know she'd lost a baby?

"In the waiting room," Luke said, "you agreed she couldn't have killed him."

Cornell's gaze flicked to where Luke held Caroline's hand. "I agreed she couldn't have shot him. But that doesn't mean that she doesn't know who did. Her husband was a billionaire. That gives me a billion reasons she might be involved in his death somehow. And the evidence the doctor just showed us is pretty convincing. What better motive to kill her husband than because he'd abused her and caused her to miscarry?"

His argument was sound. But Caroline had come to Luke asking for his help, and here she was in a hospital bed fighting for her life. She needed someone else to fight for her now. Since no one else was volunteering for the job, that someone might as well be him.

"Do you even know if she'll inherit?" he asked. "If not, that blows your billion-reason theory away."

"Not yet. I called the husband's law firm. His lawyer is going to send me a copy of the will." The detective looked at Luke's hand on Caroline's again. "Tell me, Mr. Dawson. With her resources, how hard do you think it would be for Mrs. Ashton to hire someone to kill her husband?"

Luke wanted to deny the possibility but couldn't. What Cornell said made sense. If Caroline had finally decided enough was enough, she had all the resources to make it happen.

# Chapter Four

Luke shifted in his chair, bracing his forearms on his knees as he watched the doctor and nurses on the other side of Caroline's hospital room. She'd responded well to the antibiotics and was already out of the Intensive Care Unit. Now the doctor was lightening her sedation to bring her out of her deep, healing sleep. For the first time since the discovery of Richard Ashton's body, Luke was going to be able to talk to Caroline. He looked forward to seeing her open her eyes, but he also dreaded the pain she might suffer if she hadn't known about the baby.

All but one of the nurses left the room. The remaining nurse sat in a chair beside the bed. The doctor spoke to her in low tones before approaching Luke.

"It won't be long now," he said. "Nurse Kennery will stay and monitor Mrs. Ashton until she wakes up, but I don't expect any problems."

Luke rose and shook his hand. "Thank you, Doctor."

He nodded and left the room.

Luke started toward the bed to check on Caroline, when the door opened again.

A rail-thin woman in a coal-black suit jacket and skirt hurried inside, her high heels clicking against the hard floor. She stopped when she saw Luke, her brows rising.

"Who are you?" she demanded.

He positioned himself between her and the bed. "Who are *you?*" he countered.

If anything, her brows arched even higher. "Leslie Harrison, Mrs. Ashton's attorney and friend. I know you aren't family, so again, who are you and what are you doing in her room?"

"I'm a friend," he said, not seeing any reason to tell her otherwise.

She snorted. "Caroline doesn't have any friends."

"I thought you were her friend."

Her lips compressed.

"Interesting friend," he continued. "She's been in the hospital for several days and this is the first time I've seen you here."

She opened her mouth to say something, but a moan from the bed stopped her.

The nurse rose from her chair to check on the patient.

Caroline's face tightened as if she was in pain, but her eyes remained closed.

Deciding the game of one-upmanship wasn't worth playing, Luke introduced himself. "I'm Luke Dawson. Mrs. Ashton hired me as her bodyguard. I was with her when we discovered her husband's body."

A look of surprise flashed across the lawyer's face. "She hired a bodyguard?"

"Yes. Apparently, she realized she was in danger. But apparently…you didn't? Did you know about the abuse?"

The only change in her expression was a subtle tightening of the tiny lines at the corners of her eyes.

*She did know.*

"How long?" he demanded.

"How long what?"

"How long did you know she was being beaten by her husband? And why didn't you report him to the police?"

"None of this is any of your business," she snapped. "Get out, Mr. Dawson. I'm the closest thing in this town to family that Caroline has, and I assure you if I have to call Security, they'll take my side—someone who has known her for years—over the side of a man she hired a few days ago. I'm her attorney and the executor of the late Mr. Ashton's estate. I have every right to be here. You have none. I repeat, get out."

The nurse looked back and forth between them. Behind her, Caroline's brow furrowed again, and her lips whitened. She was obviously in pain. The tug-of-war between Luke and the lawyer was distracting the nurse from taking care of her.

"All right," Luke said. "I'll go. For now. Just make sure that when you speak to Mrs. Ashton you warn her not to talk to the police without a criminal attorney present— not a civil attorney like yourself. The police are investigating her as a suspect and could misconstrue anything she says."

"I assure you, I don't need your advice about how to take care of my client." Leslie swept past him to the nurse and peppered her with questions.

Luke reluctantly left the room. He might have lost this battle, but he wasn't leaving Caroline alone for long. He'd never met Leslie Harrison before, but he didn't get good vibes from her. And her lack of concern for her alleged friend showed in the fact that she hadn't visited or called since Caroline had been brought into the emergency room. She didn't strike him as the kind of friend Caroline needed right now.

He took the elevator to the first floor and went outside to use his cell phone. The man he needed to talk to wasn't someone he spoke to very often. In fact, it had been years since the last time their paths had crossed, so he had to call a few friends to ferret out the unlisted number. Finally, he programmed it into his phone and pressed the call button.

The phone rang twice. Then, "Alex Buchanan."

"Alex, this is Luke Dawson."

"Luke." His voice mirrored his surprise. "Tell me you're not calling me to bail one of your clients out of jail again. I hung my hat up on that kind of work years ago."

"Not this time. I'm at Memorial University Medical Center visiting a friend. Are you still a practicing attorney, or are you retired?"

"I keep my license active, but I only take cases for family or friends."

"How about friends *of* friends?"

"Depends on who they are and what kind of trouble they're in. Who's your friend?"

"Caroline Ashton."

The phone went silent.

"Alex? You still there?"

"I'm here."

"Well? Will you help or not?"

A deep sigh sounded through the phone. "Bring me up to speed while I dust off a suit."

THE NURSE HELPED Caroline hobble from the bathroom to the bed. The pain in Caroline's belly was much better than before, so she wasn't about to complain at the sharp jolt that shot through her when the nurse helped her swing her feet up onto the bed. She drew several shallow breaths until the twinge passed, then collapsed against the pillows.

"Are you sure you're ready for your friend to come back inside?" the nurse asked, patting Caroline's hand and looking at her with concern. "The doctor's visit really seemed to wear you out. If you want to rest a bit, I can make sure no one bothers you."

She shook her head. "No, I'm okay. Please tell Leslie she can come back in now."

"Very well. She's in the waiting room. I'll tell her. But if she overtires you, or if the pain gets worse, press the call button."

"I will. Thank you."

The nurse left. A few minutes later the *tap-tap* of Leslie's heels sounded outside the room. The door opened and she burst inside, with three men following her.

Caroline clutched the sheets as Leslie and a stranger she'd never met moved to her left side, while the remaining two men—Daniel and Grant, her husband's brothers—caged her in on the other side of the bed.

"Leslie, I don't understand," she whispered. "Why are Daniel and Grant here?"

"Our brother is dead," Grant sneered. "We have a right to find out what happened."

Leslie's lip curled with distaste. "Unfortunately, they were in the waiting room, demanding to see you. When Detective Cornell and I headed here, they followed like lapdogs."

Grant looked as if he wanted to leap across the bed and take a swing at Leslie. Daniel's face turned a light shade of pink, as if he was embarrassed at his brother's behavior.

The man beside Leslie held up his hand. "Quiet, everyone. Mrs. Ashton, I'm Detective Cornell with Chatham County Metro P.D. If you're feeling up to it, I have some questions for you." He glanced at the others, the look on his face showing displeasure. "Your family insisted on coming in with me, but I can ask them to step outside.

Or, if you prefer," he said, his voice sounding grudging, "I can wait in the hall until you speak to them privately."

"No." She winced at how loud her voice sounded in the small room. "That is, I'd prefer not to have these other men here, if that's okay."

"We're not going anywhere," Grant said.

"Yes. You are." Luke Dawson's deep voice rang out from the open doorway. He strode inside and stopped at the foot of Caroline's bed, frowning at Cornell and Leslie before looking at the other two men. "You heard her. Out."

Grant drew himself up, but even so, he was still an inch shorter than Luke and not nearly as broad. "Our brother was murdered," he snapped, aiming a glare at Caroline. "And we have the right to hear what *she* has to say about it."

Luke moved so fast it stole Caroline's breath. One minute he was standing there, calmly eyeing Grant. The next minute he had Grant's arm wedged up between his shoulder blades. Grant's face was bright red, but he didn't seem to be able to move.

"Let me go, you stupid rent-a-cop," he gasped.

"I'll let you go—outside." Luke raised a challenging brow at Daniel, daring him to intervene.

Daniel glared at Luke before heading to the door. Luke followed, pushing Grant ahead of him. The door softly closed behind them.

Cornell pulled a plastic chair to the side of the bed and sat. "I take it you aren't close to your brothers-in-law?"

Caroline shook her head. "No. I definitely don't consider them…family. And I assure you, the feeling is mutual."

The door clicked back open and Luke hurried inside, stopping at the foot of the bed again.

"Mrs. Ashton, if you don't want me here, I'll wait in the hallway." He looked pointedly at the detective and Leslie. "But I thought you might want one ally in your corner, something you seem to have little of at the moment. I also strongly urge you not to say anything to Detective Cornell without a lawyer. A *criminal* lawyer, not a civil one."

Leslie pursed her lips but didn't say anything.

"Cornell isn't here with your best interests at heart," Luke continued. "He considers you a suspect in your husband's murder."

Caroline blinked at the detective. His face reddened, telling her Luke's words were true.

"I'm not your enemy," Cornell explained. "I simply want to know what happened. But first, I'd like to offer you my condolences on the death of your husband."

She shivered and rubbed her hands up and down her arms. Even though she knew Richard was dead, hearing it out loud didn't make it seem real. She kept expecting him to pounce at her from behind the curtains, or stride out of the bathroom and laugh at her for thinking she could ever escape him.

"Thank you, Detective."

"Have you had a chance to speak to your doctor yet?"

"Yes," she whispered. "He was here a few moments ago."

"Then you know he suspects your husband abused you, that he's the reason for your fractures, bruises, your ruptured spleen...your miscarriage?"

She winced and automatically moved her hand to her belly. "Yes. He told me."

"Is it true? Did your husband beat you?"

She blanched, her face growing hot. She'd never wanted

anyone else to know about her shame. Until a few days ago, no one did. No one but Leslie.

"I don't want to talk about this."

"It's the elephant in the room," Cornell continued. "It can't be avoided. You hired a bodyguard, Mr. Dawson here. Why did you hire him?"

She glanced at Luke. "I knew my husband would be angry that I'd left him. And I didn't want to have to deal with an argument. I wanted someone who could confront him, if necessary, and save me from the ugliness."

"Are you denying your husband hurt you?" the detective asked.

She twisted her fingers in the sheets. "I don't—"

"Don't say another word," Luke said. "You need a criminal defense attorney before you speak to the police."

Leslie patted Caroline's hand. "The sooner she answers the questions, the sooner this will all be over and she can put it behind her. Perhaps it would be best if you waited outside, Mr. Dawson."

"Not a chance."

"No," Caroline said at the same time. She pulled her hand back from Leslie's. "I'm sorry, but I feel…better with Mr. Dawson here. Detective Cornell, all I can tell you is that I didn't kill my husband. I don't own a gun. I don't even think Richard owned one. There was no need, not with a security firm watching over the house. And regardless of what Richard did or didn't do, I never wanted him dead."

"I agree it appears you couldn't have killed him yourself, based on the timeline of events and the witnesses to your whereabouts. But that doesn't mean you didn't hire someone else to kill him."

Her mouth fell open. "Why would I do that?"

"Your husband was quite wealthy. Maybe you figured you wouldn't get much if you divorced him." He cocked his head and studied her. "Was there a prenuptial agreement limiting how much you would get in a divorce?"

"Yes. There was. But I didn't care. I was leaving my husband, regardless of the money."

Cornell didn't look impressed by her statement. He scribbled something in his notepad. "I think when you decided to leave your husband, you didn't want to lose the money. You called a friend, maybe a lover, offered him a portion of the estate if he'd help you stage your husband's murder to make it look like you had nothing to do with it. Who helped you?"

She laughed bitterly. "A friend? A lover? My husband made sure I had no one, Detective. I didn't make a move that he didn't know about. I couldn't even leave the house without him."

"Obviously that's not true. You left without him Thursday morning."

She rolled her head on the pillow. "The one thing my husband allowed me to do on my own, the *only* thing he let me do, was run two weekly errands—taking our clothes to the dry cleaner's and bringing his papers to his lawyer's office, to Leslie's office. That's what I was doing. That's how I left without him knowing I was taking off."

"'Let' you?" the detective asked. "Are you saying you were a prisoner in your own home? Did you resent your husband for controlling you that way?"

"That's enough." Luke said. "Mrs. Ashton, again, I strongly urge you not to say another word without adequate legal representation."

The door flew open. A tall man in a business suit stepped into the room. His coal-black hair had tiny streaks of silver, but that was the only thing that hinted at his age. His blue eyes were still vivid, piercing, as they swept the room and landed on her.

"And just who the devil are you?" Leslie demanded.

Luke looked relieved to see the other man.

The man ignored Leslie, nodded at Luke. He stepped to the side of Caroline's bed and smiled down at her. "I'm Alex Buchanan, a defense attorney with one of the best records in the state of Georgia. Mr. Dawson called me about your situation. And from where I stand, you look like you could use my help." He pulled a dollar out of his suit-jacket pocket and handed it to her.

"What's this for?" she asked, automatically taking it.

"I figure you probably don't have any cash with you here in the hospital. If you'd like me to represent you, you can give me that dollar as my retainer."

Leslie scoffed.

Cornell's mouth curved in grudging admiration.

Caroline looked at Luke. "You think I need help?"

"I know you do. Alex really is the best. I recommend that you hire him."

She held the dollar out to the handsome man smiling down at her. "You're hired, Mr. Buchanan."

He took the dollar and slid it back into his pocket. "Excellent. Detective Cornell, miss," he said, looking at Leslie. "I need a moment alone with my client."

"I'm not leaving unless he does," Leslie said, pointing at Luke.

Alex smiled without humor. "Yes, you are. You're both leaving. But Mr. Dawson stays. Three days ago, someone killed my client's husband. And if she'd arrived at the house a few moments earlier, she could have been killed, as well. Mr. Dawson is her bodyguard. He's not going anywhere."

APPARENTLY, CAROLINE LOVED GARDENS. Luke had done his best to find one for her so she, Alex and he could talk without anyone overhearing them. The closest thing to a garden the hospital had was a spot in a small, empty waiting room on the first floor that looked out a group of windows to some flowering shrubs.

Not that it really mattered. Caroline wasn't paying attention to the view. She sat in her wheelchair staring at Alex with the same confusion Luke felt.

"I don't understand," she said.

Luke shook his head. "Neither do I. Maybe you should explain one more time, Alex. How, exactly, am I supposed to protect Caroline when I won't even be in the house with her?"

"Mrs. Ashton already has a contract with a security company to guard the mansion. Stellar Security has an excellent record. There's no reason to believe they can't take care of her without your help."

"If you truly believe that, then why am I even here?" Luke asked.

"To protect Mrs. Ashton."

Caroline's brow furrowed and she shared another look of confusion with Luke.

"See, that's the part where you lost me earlier," Luke said.

Alex smiled. "Forgive me. I'm not explaining this very well. Based on my current understanding of the case, we only know one thing—that someone murdered Mr. Ashton. We don't know if the killer wanted to kill him, or if Mrs. Ashton was his true target, or if it was simply a burglary gone wrong with no real connection to either of the Ashtons."

"I hadn't thought of that," Caroline said.

"I'm sure Detective Cornell has, but he confronted

you earlier to shake you up, to see your reaction. Right now, everyone has more questions than answers. What I want to do is keep the status quo, keep the variables as close to normal as possible. That will make it much more obvious if someone has changed their routine, or if they act differently. By returning to your usual routine, it will be easier to judge people's reactions, easier to point out if someone seems a bit...off."

Luke tapped the table. "And I'm supposed to sit in my car and watch the mansion? What good does that do?"

"It allows you to become invisible. No one is going to pay attention to you outside, but if you're inside, everyone acts differently and it will be much harder for Mrs. Ashton to pick up on any changes."

"Please call me Caroline, both of you. And as far as your plan, Alex, I agree it will be fairly easy for me to spot any changes that way."

"I'm concerned about your safety," Luke insisted.

"There's no reason to believe Mrs. Ashton's...that is, Caroline's security company that's already in place can't continue to protect the mansion. Stellar Security has an unblemished reputation."

"You're right. They do. Caroline, as much as it galls me to admit it, you probably don't need me anymore."

She reached for his hand. From the way her eyes widened, it appeared she was just as surprised at her action as Luke was, but he didn't pull away. Instead, he threaded his fingers with hers.

Some of the tension went out of her and she gave him a tentative smile. "It may not seem like I need you, but I do. The mansion has never been my home. No one there is my friend or cares one whit about me. While I'd prefer that you be inside, with me, just knowing you are watching over the place will give me comfort. That is, if you don't mind."

He considered the hours he'd be spending sitting in his car. He wouldn't be able to run the air conditioner all that time, not without overheating the engine, which meant *he'd* be the one overheating. That thought should have had him wanting to end the contract and go back to his office. But it didn't. For some reason, he couldn't bear not being there. He wanted, needed, to make sure she really was safe.

"If that's what you want, then I'm happy to stay on the case, in whatever capacity you and Alex think makes sense."

She smiled and pulled her hand back.

Luke sorely missed the feel of her delicate hand in his, which surprised him again. Everything about Caroline and his reactions to her surprised him.

Alex raised a brow at the exchange but didn't comment on it.

"What about Leslie?" Caroline asked Alex. "You mentioned earlier you had concerns about her."

"I do. Tell me, how did you end up renting the cottage where your husband was killed?"

"Leslie helped me find it on the internet."

"Did she know what time you were supposed to arrive on the day you were moving in?"

"Well, yes." Her eyes widened. "You can't be suggesting she had anything to do with Richard's death."

"Not suggesting," Alex said. "Just exploring the facts. She knew where you were going and what time you'd be there, so you have to consider she could have planned the murder expecting you to discover the body. She may have wanted you to look guilty."

Caroline shook her head. "No, that's not what happened at all. Leslie had nothing to gain from Richard's death. And she couldn't have known what time I'd be at the cottage because I changed plans after leaving her office. I hired Luke. Then I went to the house."

Luke exchanged a look with Alex. From the expression on Alex's face, Luke realized they were both thinking the same thing. Luke shifted forward in his chair. "Caroline, you changed plans, but Leslie didn't know that, did she? What exactly did she think you were going to do after leaving her office?"

Her lips compressed into a tight line. She obviously didn't appreciate where the conversation was going. "She was just looking out for my safety. She didn't want Richard to find me. We both agreed I would go directly to the rental."

"And if you had done that," Luke said, "you would have arrived right about the time your husband was shot. It sounds to me like you wouldn't have had an alibi if you had done what your lawyer expected you to do."

The resentment on her face faded as the truth hung in the air between them.

She swallowed hard. "Leslie did stress that I needed to go directly to the cottage, that I shouldn't stop anywhere. But that doesn't mean she had anything to do with Richard's death. You're suggesting she might have wanted to frame me. What would she gain from that?"

Alex shook his head. "I have no idea. But we need to look at all the possibilities. I have other concerns about Miss Harrison. She's a tax attorney, but she still took the same oath I did. She knows that protecting her clients is her first priority. And by allowing you to speak to the police without a criminal-law attorney present, she displayed incredibly poor judgment, at the least. I'd like you to be careful around her until the investigation can clear her of any involvement. You can still keep her in your normal routine, but don't sign anything or agree to anything without vetting it through me first. See if she does anything to raise red flags with you."

"Okay, but I can tell you there's no reason to be concerned. Leslie is the only friend I have. She's the one who helped me get the cottage and helped me plan leaving my husband."

Alex crossed his arms. "How long did she know about the abuse?"

Caroline's gaze fell to her lap. "About six months."

Luke cursed.

Alex looked as if he wanted to do the same, but he refrained. "As a lawyer, it was Miss Harrison's obligation to help you. While she may not have been legally bound to report the abuse like a doctor would be, she's ethically and morally bound to do so. I assure you, her turning a blind eye—even if she helped you later on—would not look well for her if she came up for review before the bar."

"I don't want her to get in trouble," Caroline said. "Whether you agree with her methods or not, she's the only one who ever tried to help me, the only person who ever seemed to notice there was anything wrong. Without her, I would never have figured out how to escape."

"How long was the abuse going on?" Alex asked.

Her face went pale. "Years."

"Then why now? After all that time, what made you decide it was time to leave?"

"The baby," she whispered. "As soon as I realized I was pregnant, I decided I had to figure out a way to get out of there. I couldn't risk bringing up a child in that environment. I may have been weak and a coward when it came to myself, but I couldn't do that to a child. I started making plans that same day." She closed her eyes. "But before everything was finalized, Richard…taught me one of his…lessons. The cramping, the bleeding…I knew I'd lost the baby. I was so ashamed. I couldn't allow myself to risk getting pregnant again, risk the life of another child."

Luke took her hand in his. "Stop talking like that. You aren't weak, or a coward. You were in an untenable situation. I understand the cycle of abuse. I've seen it over and over. It's not easy to get out. Your abuser plays a mind game on you, slowly wearing you down until one day you don't even know how you got in the place where you're at. It's not your fault. None of this. It's Richard Ashton's fault. And you didn't kill your child. He did."

Unshed tears made her eyes bright. She gave him a watery smile. "Thank you."

He squeezed her hand in answer.

Alex frowned. "I'm sure Miss Harrison has filed your husband's will with the courts by now, but I'm new to this case and don't have the particulars. Can you give me a summary? Who are Mr. Ashton's beneficiaries?"

"His brothers and me."

"Split equally?"

"No. For some reason, Richard decided to leave me the bulk of the estate. He left five million to each of his brothers, but everything else goes to me."

"Did he get along with his brothers?"

"More with Daniel than Grant, but he fought with both of them off and on over the years. Daniel hasn't been to the house in quite some time, but I don't know if he and Richard were fighting or not. Grant comes over more often, but his visits usually end in some kind of argument. He and Richard seem to have…issues. They came to blows on occasion. Richard was definitely the type to hold a grudge, so maybe that explains why he didn't leave much—relative to the entire estate, of course—to Grant.

But I thought Richard and Daniel had a better relationship overall. I don't understand why he left Daniel so little."

"Forgive me," Alex said, "but I have to ask because you can bet the police will. If you'd divorced, was there an agreement in place about what you would have received?"

"Yes. Two hundred thousand dollars a year, for life. I was never worried about the money. Trust me, that kind of money would have been plenty."

"A jury might feel differently. That's a drastic change in lifestyle for someone who's used to being in a mansion, married to a billionaire." He shrugged. "Those are the facts. We'll just have to deal with them."

Luke leaned forward in his chair. "Let's get back to the plan for how to keep her safe until the killer is caught. I'm all for assuming she's as much a target as her husband. I'd rather be too cautious than to let down my guard. First thing to consider—what do we do about the funeral for Mr. Ashton?"

# Chapter Five

It nearly killed Luke being outside Caroline's inner circle, relying on Alex's instincts that she'd be safe with her usual bodyguards, at least for now. But he did as Alex had suggested. The plan the defense lawyer had put in place seemed solid. And Alex had hired a private investigator to dig into everything on the side to bolster Caroline's defense, if that became necessary, and also to try to find out the identity of the killer.

The investigator was also digging into Leslie Harrison's past to see if she had anything to gain by either framing Caroline, or by having her killed along with Richard if Caroline had arrived at the cottage when Leslie expected her to that day.

Luke watched the hospital entrance from his 1997 Ford Thunderbird parked between two tall SUVs that made it less likely anyone would notice him. Not that they would anyway. Few people stopped to admire his olive-green, beat-up car, which was exactly how he wanted it. This was his work car, built like a tank, dented and scratched from run-ins when the people he was protecting his clients from decided to come after him instead. He even had several spare tires in the trunk instead of the traditional "one," prepared for the next time someone decided to slash his tires.

But worrying about some pimp coming after him wasn't on his mind today. Caroline was. She was being released from the hospital. And her husband's funeral was being held today. Alex had advised her to go to the funeral, whether she wanted to or not, saying it would look bad if she didn't attend. If things didn't go her way and she ended up in court, accused of orchestrating her husband's murder, her not being at the funeral might poison the jury against her. So here she was, about to leave the hospital and having to pay homage to the man who'd put her there in the first place.

The idea made Luke sick and wish he could bring the bastard back from the dead and kill him himself.

The parking lot around him was filled with media vans. As soon as the Ashton Rolls-Royce pulled up the circular driveway to the front of the hospital, reporters converged on them like a swarm of mosquitoes.

His cell phone vibrated on the seat beside him. He glanced at the screen, then put it on speaker. "Hey, Mitch."

"You still at the hospital?"

"Sitting out front. The Ashton limo just drove up. She should be out soon. Are you in position?"

"I've got the best spot in the cemetery picked out. Not close enough to the party to be obvious, but close enough to observe and photograph everyone who shows up. I'm starting to like this P.I. stuff. You might have to expand the business and make me lead detective."

"Guess that depends on how well you do today. I'd say don't make a scene taking pictures, but with the media horde that will be there, you aren't going to stand out anyway. Alex will have someone there taking pictures, too. Between the both of you, if Alex's theory that the killer will be there is true, we'll at least have him or her

on camera and be able to start a list of potential suspects."
He shook his head at the crowd of reporters trying to get
past the police line at the hospital for a better angle for
their cameras. "Then again, counting the press, we'll
probably have hundreds of people to look into."

"Doesn't bother me at all. Like I said, I'm enjoying
this. It's a heck of a lot better than sitting in the office
all day."

"Speaking of which, who's looking after things while
you're playing amateur sleuth?"

"Trudy."

Luke squeezed the bridge of his nose. "You've got my
business being watched over by a hooker?"

"Ex-hooker. She's gone respectable, trying to make a
living with her feet on the ground for a change."

"Since when?"

"Well…playing office secretary might be her first real
gig, but I think it's great for us to give her a start toward
a better life, don't you?"

Luke rolled his head on his shoulders, trying to relieve
the growing knot of tension. He was all for helping the
less fortunate, but not at the expense of his livelihood.

He was about to set Mitch straight when the passenger
door to the limo opened and one of the Ashton-estate security guards got out. The hospital doors swished open.
Out came Caroline Ashton, looking extra pale in a con-
servative black dress, being pushed in a wheelchair by
a nurse. Beside her was her so-called friend Leslie Harrison. A bevy of security guards surrounded them both,
preventing any of the reporters from getting near her.
Luke had to admit that he was impressed with how Stellar Security had handled the situation.

"I've got to go. They're helping Mrs. Ashton into the
limo. After the burial, get those pictures straight to Alex."

"You got it, boss."

Luke ended the call and eased out of the parking lot, keeping well back from the Rolls-Royce and the caravan of press hounds sniffing in its wake.

HUNDREDS OF PEOPLE who'd worked for Richard at his various companies turned out for the viewing at the funeral home. Caroline tried to be gracious as she sat up front and accepted their condolences. But it was hard to smile and listen to so many people who had such wonderful stories to tell about her husband, when she'd seen so little of that warmth as his wife.

By the time the viewing was closed and everyone had filed out except the funeral director and security guards, and, of course, Leslie—who didn't seem inclined to ever leave her side—Caroline's nerves were stretched so tight she thought she might start screaming like the madwoman so many people believed her to be.

"Caroline, we should go now or we'll be late for the burial," Leslie said.

Leslie's worries seemed silly with the coffin sitting a few feet away. They couldn't hold a funeral without the guest of honor.

She hadn't gone near the coffin with everyone else there. At first, she had assumed she wouldn't want to, but now, knowing this was the last time she'd ever see him, she had the sudden urge to do so.

"I'd like a few moments alone, please."

Leslie frowned. "But we need to—"

"I need a few moments alone," she repeated and looked pointedly at the security guard closest to her.

Leslie's brows rose, but she got up as the guard stopped in front of her. She gave Caroline an irritated look and left the room.

Once all the guards were gone, she sat for several moments, trying to gather her courage.

A whisper of sound had her turning her head. Luke Dawson, dressed in a black suit, moved up the aisle and sat beside her. He put his hand on the wooden bench seat, palm up, an unspoken offer of friendship and support. She didn't hesitate. She put her hand in his.

"I'd hoped you'd come," she said.

"I gave you a promise that I'd keep you safe. In spite of what Alex recommends, I can't seem to stay that far away from you." He inclined his head toward the coffin. "If you want me to leave, I will."

Her hand tightened on his. "No. I'm glad you're here. Would you mind…standing with me?"

"Whatever you need." He helped her to her feet.

She was still wobbly and weak. She would use the wheelchair later, at the graveside service, but right now—with the coffin open—it was almost as if her husband could still see her. She knew it didn't make sense, but she didn't want to use the wheelchair here so she wouldn't look weak in front of him.

Luke's strong arm was her rock to cling to as she slowly approached the coffin.

She stared down at the man she'd married, and a shiver ran through her. Luke placed his arm around her shoulders and drew her against his side. Somehow that action helped stave off her panic and allowed her to do what she really wanted to do—face the monster and say goodbye to the man the monster had once been, the man she'd fallen in love with.

Tears coursed down her cheeks. "I'm sure to someone like you, just knowing about the awful things he did to me, you can't imagine why I'd cry. But he wasn't always the man you've heard about. When I met him, he was my savior. He took me from a life of poverty, from an unhappy home, and gave me a fresh start. He was so handsome, and strong, and his smile…I felt it all the way to my heart. I truly, deeply loved him, before…before he…changed."

Luke gently stroked her upper arm. "You don't owe me, or anyone else, any explanations."

The lack of judgment and condemnation in his voice dramatically highlighted the differences between these two men. Where Luke treated her with respect and tried to build her up, Richard had only sought to break her down with his constant criticism and humiliating lessons.

She blinked back her tears. Crying wouldn't soothe the hurt deep in her heart, or heal the ache for the man he'd once been and the man he'd ultimately become. Only time would do that—or, at least, she hoped so.

Luke stood well back from the group of mourners and security guards and police officers, the latter there mostly to keep the press from mobbing the graveside service. A dark green tent covered the casket and the thirty or so white folding chairs that were all occupied, with many mourners standing at the edge of the tent, spilling onto the green grass.

Luke stood in the cover of oak trees, scanning the crowd, watching for anything that didn't seem right. Normally he performed bodyguard services right beside the person he was guarding. Watching over Caroline long-distance didn't sit well. It didn't sit well at all. But, again, the guards with Stellar Security seemed to be doing a good job of keeping everyone back and keeping a ring of their men around Caroline. If the killer was here, and wanted to get at her, he'd have a tough go of it.

Satisfied that Caroline was being well protected, he

scanned the crowd to find Mitch. There, on the top of a knoll, separated from the closest group of media hounds by about ten feet, Mitch snapped pictures with a big grin on his face. Luke wryly wondered if Mitch had found his true calling in life. He certainly never looked that happy at the office.

Using his binoculars to search the crowd, Luke located Alex and was surprised to see him standing beside Leslie Harrison. The two of them had no love for each other. Maybe Alex was trying to get in Leslie's good graces to extract information from her.

Screams sounded from the crowd. Luke focused on the tent. He couldn't find Caroline. Panic squeezed his throat. But then he saw her being carried in the arms of one of her guards, with the rest of the guards circling her, guns drawn, ready for any threat. As soon as she was in the car, the caravan of security vehicles raced away.

Another scream rent the air. Luke whirled around, urgently searching for the other people he knew. He located them, one by one—first Leslie, unhurt, running toward the parking lot. Then Alex, at her side, using his tall, muscular frame to protect her. One more person to find. He scanned back and forth over the area where Mitch had been just moments ago.

A small crowd had gathered on a slight rise. Luke zoomed in, trying to see why they were all looking down. He sucked in a sharp breath. It was a body, deathly still, blood seeping through his shirt. A camera lay like a forgotten trophy beside him. *Mitch.*

*No!* Luke drew his gun and tore off in a sprint, desperately offering up a prayer as he ran.

AN HOUR LATER, Caroline sat with Alex on one side of the table in the interview room at the police station, while

Luke sat alone on the other end, stone-faced, pale, his lips drawn into a tight line. Cornell sat in the middle.

"I'm very sorry for your loss, Mr. Dawson," Cornell said.

Luke gave him a curt nod.

Alex clasped Luke's shoulder, expressing his sympathy in silence before dropping his hand.

"I'm sorry, too," Caroline whispered.

Luke's dark gaze fastened onto hers. "I know. It's not your fault." His eyes narrowed. "You realize that, right?"

She looked away.

"Caroline?" he repeated, his voice raw but insistent. "You're not the one who stabbed him. It's not your fault."

She nodded, since he seemed to be waiting for an answer.

"Did Mr. Brody have family we can notify?" Cornell asked.

A pained expression crossed Luke's face. For a moment Caroline thought he was going to break down. But, instead, he straightened his shoulders, as if to brace himself against giving in to his grief.

"No. He was homeless when I met him. No family, no education to speak of. I'm all he had." His last sentence came out a stark whisper.

Caroline's guilt nearly choked her. Luke had taken Mitch in and given him a new life. And now—because of her—his friend was dead. She twisted her hands together in her lap.

"There will be an autopsy, of course," Cornell said. "But the cause of death is obvious. Someone stabbed him in the back. He bled out. As far as a burial—"

"Give the coroner my contact information," Luke said. "I'll make the arrangements."

"Very well. I know this is a tough time, but did any of you see anything?"

All three of them shook their heads.

"Okay. We'll examine the pictures from his camera. Maybe something will come of that. We don't actually know if this is related in any way to Mr. Ashton's murder, but I have to believe it's a strong possibility. Mrs. Ashton, are you sure you've never met Mitch Brody before?"

She glanced at Alex. He nodded, letting her know it was okay to answer.

"Not until last Thursday, when I picked Dawson's Personal Security Services out of the phone book."

"Okay. At this point I recommend that each of you be extra careful. Until we figure out what we're up against, everyone is a suspect. Watch your backs."

## Chapter Six

Caroline paused at the front door to the mansion. A sense of foreboding swept through her. She couldn't shake the horror of Mitch being killed earlier today. She hadn't really known the man, but he'd been there because of her. His death was her fault.

No. His death was *not* her fault. She had to stop blaming herself and putting herself down the way Richard had always done. The person to blame for Mitch's death was whoever had stabbed him. She had to remember that. Richard had made her feel guilty for everything and had made her doubt her own sanity. No more. She was taking control of her own life, her own self-worth.

Still, she hesitated to go inside, in spite of the puzzled looks the security guards and Leslie were giving her. All she could picture in her mind was how strong and virile her husband had been. It was almost impossible to accept that he wasn't going to greet her at the door. She could easily imagine his outrage over her being so late in coming home, over her trying to escape. Of course, in front of others, he'd pretend to be happy to see her. He'd likely kiss her and hold her close. But in private, once the bedroom doors shut, he'd be all too eager to teach her another "lesson."

She shuddered and protectively wrapped her arms

around her middle, although it wasn't even slightly cold in the humid heat that engulfed the house.

Leslie put her hand on her shoulder. "Are you okay? Are you in pain?"

Caroline stared at the woman she thought of as her friend, looking for some sign that she really *wasn't* her friend, that she might have had something to do with Richard's murder as Alex and Luke had theorized.

"Caroline?" Leslie's brows drew together.

"No, I'm not in pain." Caroline hated that she had these doubts about the woman who'd done so much to help her. "I was just…thinking."

One of the security guards opened the door and stood back for them to enter.

She braced herself, then stepped into the foyer with Leslie at her side, only to be greeted by three maids and the cook. Or rather, they greeted Leslie and ignored Caroline. Which was just as well because she didn't want to deal with their red-rimmed eyes and sniffles. Richard was beloved by the staff, and it looked as if they were taking his death hard.

The security guards locked the door and melted into the house as they always did, somewhere out of sight but ready to help when needed—except, of course, when Caroline had really needed help, when Richard was around.

The household staff gathered around Leslie, whom they'd all met on numerous occasions, and offered her their condolences, completely ignoring their employer's widow, who just so happened to now be their *employer*.

Suddenly it was all too much. The miscarriage, two severe beatings in two days, finally escaping Richard only to find him murdered, winding up in the hospital with sepsis and having emergency surgery, and then for young, innocent Mitch Brody to be killed at the cemetery—all of it had her nerves stretched to the snapping point.

Someone was either trying to kill her or pin her for murder. And after everything she'd been through, it was so unfair. Well, she wasn't putting up with "unfair" anymore. She'd taken a huge step escaping Richard. Now it was time to take another huge step, to set her house in order. Because now this house was *hers*. Not Richard's. Not the staff's. And it was high time they treated her with the same respect they treated everyone else—starting now.

"Karen, Missy, Natasha, Betsy," she said, enjoying the startled looks on the other women's faces. They weren't used to being addressed by her directly. They probably didn't even think she knew their names. "I appreciate your condolences and that you all miss my husband, but life must go on. Your time is best spent performing your duties. Betsy, will you please arrange for my belongings to be moved out of the master suite into the main guest bedroom?"

Betsy looked from Leslie to Caroline. "I, um… Ma'am, why would you want me to do that?"

Caroline fisted her hands at her sides. She shouldn't have to explain to this woman who'd treated her as if she didn't exist for the past five years that her husband had repeatedly beaten and raped her in the master bedroom and she would never, ever step foot in that hated room again.

"If you have a problem following my orders, then I suggest you look for employment elsewhere." She looked in turn at all four women, who were huddled together as if they thought she was crazy. "That goes for all of you. Things are going to change, starting today. I refuse to be invisible in my own home any longer. I'm your employer. If you can't live with that, you are welcome to leave."

She brushed past the women, her shoulders straight

and her head held high, pretending a confidence she was far from feeling. She stepped through the nearest doorway, then abruptly stopped and pressed her hand to her throat. The enormous wood-paneled room at the front of the house looked out over the circular driveway. The view was unfamiliar because she'd only caught glimpses of it before. This was Richard's office, a room he'd forbidden her to enter. She could look through the doorway, on those occasions when her husband needed to speak to her, but she could never step inside. She turned around, intending to leave, but Leslie and the others were in the foyer staring at her.

She straightened her spine. "Leslie, are you coming or not?"

"Um, yes, of course." She clutched her purse and followed Caroline into the room.

Caroline raised a brow at the women in the foyer.

They scurried away, like chickens running from a fox. She grinned, pleased with the image. It was nice to be the fox for a change, instead of the chicken. She shut the door with a decisive click.

Her smile died when she saw the look on Leslie's face. "What? Did I do something wrong?"

Leslie set her purse on a decorative table and sat on the couch in the grouping at one end of the room. A massive walnut desk sat on the other side, next to the wall of windows. Caroline steered clear of the desk and sat in one of the leather wing chairs beside the couch.

"Not wrong, exactly," Leslie said. "I just don't think you should bait the staff and talk about changes so quickly after Richard was killed. You're still on the potential-suspect list. We wouldn't want anyone to get the idea you were glad Richard is dead."

"Is that what you think? That I'm glad he's dead?"

"Aren't you?"

She thought back to Alex's warning to keep everything the same as much as possible, to flush out anyone who might act out of the ordinary. But in spite of his recommendations, she couldn't pretend to be sorry. She was tired of being invisible in her own house.

"I'm glad I don't have to be afraid anymore. That's what I'm glad about. But I would never take comfort in someone's death, not even Richard's."

"Admirable of you, my dear. Just be careful not to give anyone the wrong impression."

Caroline bit her lip. "I suppose I did come on a bit strong." She shook her head. "No. I'm not sorry I took charge. I've been living like a turtle afraid of its own shell for too long. I'm determined not to live that way anymore. I've been given a second chance. I'm not going to waste a single minute of it."

She crossed to Richard's most prized possession, his sacred desk. She plopped down in the leather chair that practically swallowed her up and crossed her arms on top of the meticulously polished surface. Unable to suppress a childish urge, she pressed her palm against the dark wood, leaving a smeared print.

Leslie's brows rose and she crossed to sit in one of the two chairs in front of the desk. "This sounds ominous. What do you intend to do, exactly?"

Caroline laughed, and because it felt so good, she laughed again. "I don't know. I suppose, to start, I just might fire the security firm that Richard hired. Yes, I think I will."

Leslie's eyes widened. "Why would you do that?"

She clasped her hands tightly together on the desk, her mood plummeting as the recent past pressed down upon her.

"I haven't told you half of what I went through living here with Richard. And I have no intention of sharing those details. But suffice it to say, I was a prisoner, and the security company was my jailer. They reported every movement I made."

"I understand your resentment, but again, I don't recommend that you be hasty. There are a great many Ashton properties the security company takes care of, and numerous businesses."

"I hadn't thought of that."

"Of course not. You aren't used to the world of finance and business. There's a lot to consider." Leslie took some stapled papers out of the side pocket of her purse and set them on the desk. "If you'll sign the first and last page, I can take care of the details for you, and all you'll have to worry about is what kind of clothes you'd like to go shopping for or what kind of vacation you might want to take." She smiled brightly and set a pen on top of the papers.

Caroline picked up the pen and read the heading on the first page. "'Power of attorney'? I don't understand. Why do you need this?"

"Just a formality. It allows me to continue to conduct business for Ashton Enterprises without you having to sign papers every week."

The doubts that Alex and Luke had planted in her mind about Leslie suddenly became too glaring to ignore. Something wasn't right.

"But Richard signed papers every week. He didn't give you one of these forms, did he?"

Leslie waved her hand. "No, but we both know how controlling he was. It was entirely unnecessary for him to sign papers all the time when I could have done it for him. You can avoid all that by simply endorsing this one.

I'll have Linda put her notary stamp on it back at the office to save you a trip."

Had this been Leslie's goal all along? While Caroline couldn't see her friend as a murderer, she wasn't blind to the ambition and greed the lawyer never bothered to conceal. Had Leslie planned to get Caroline to sign over control of a billion-dollar enterprise? Had she planned on Caroline being in jail and desperate at the time, so that she wouldn't think twice about signing?

Caroline set the pen down. She glanced past Leslie to the closed door, every muscle in her body going tense. She forced the safe, blank look onto her face that she'd used so many times when trying to hide her feelings from her husband.

"This is all new to me, like you said. And I want to make sure I get everything right. Will you bring me up to date on all of the Ashton holdings so I know what's what?"

Leslie frowned. "Why on earth would you want me to bore you with those details? I'll take care of everything for you."

Caroline clenched her hand beneath the desk and glanced at the door again. She forced a smile. "Have I done something to annoy you, Leslie? You sound…aggravated."

Leslie's frown smoothed out and her lips curved into an answering smile. "Of course not. I'm just worried about you. If you want to dig into the boring details of the businesses, then by all means. I'll gather the necessary reports to bring you up to speed."

"That would be nice, of course. But I'd like to start with something smaller, just the household accounts. I want to know what expenses we have and how to pay the bills. After all, that's something I need to take care of, right? And I'll have to get the banks to put me on Richard's checking accounts, savings accounts, things like that. The monthly allowance he gave me in my own account won't be sufficient to pay the costs of running this place, like the staff's payroll."

"Again, that's something I can take care of. If you'll sign—"

"Leslie. I'm not going to argue about this. It's important to me. I want to learn what I need to know to run my own life, without someone else running it for me."

Leslie pursed her lips. "Of course. I wasn't considering everything you've gone through, and that having control over such mundane things might be important to you." She reached for the papers.

Caroline pulled the papers away and slid them into the top desk drawer. "I'll keep the papers here and think about signing. Okay?"

Leslie glanced toward the drawer, not looking at all pleased. For a moment, Caroline wondered if she was going to lunge over the desk and try to grab the papers. But finally Leslie snapped her purse shut.

"I'll get what you need from the bank as well as the house account information. It will take a day or two. With it being Sunday, the bank's not open, of course. I can come back on Wednesday. I should have everything together by then."

Caroline shoved out of the chair and walked Leslie to the door. "Wednesday sounds perfect. We can have lunch out back by the pool. Wear something casual. It will be fun."

"Fun." Leslie frowned again. "I've never seen this side of you, Caroline. I must say, it's going to take a bit of getting used to."

When the front door closed behind Leslie, Caroline slumped against the wall. She ran a shaking hand through her hair and stood for several minutes until she felt calm enough to go back into Richard's office.

No, *her* office. She went inside and stood at the floor-to-ceiling windows. She closed her eyes and leaned her forehead against the glass. The energy she'd had earlier seemed to desert her now. She was tired, so tired, and the day was only half over. She had so much to do, like telling Alex and Luke about the documents Leslie had tried to get her to sign.

"Excuse me, Mrs. Ashton?"

She turned at the sound of the head maid's voice. "Hello, Natasha. I'm sorry if I was a bit…abrupt earlier."

The maid gave her an uncertain look, as if she wasn't sure Caroline was going to run shrieking from the room tearing at her hair.

Caroline sighed. "Was there something you wanted?"

"Oh, yes, ma'am." She held out a small stack of envelopes. "The mail. I usually place it on Mr. Ashton's desk, but I…wasn't sure where you might want it."

Progress already. The maid had actually asked her preference rather than ignoring her and going about her business.

Caroline smiled and took the mail. "Thank you. I feel as if I've been sleepwalking around here for quite some time. I haven't really been aware of the routines you and the others go through. I apologize for not paying attention. As clean and well run as this household is, it's obvious the staff does an amazing job."

The woman stood a little straighter and her smile reached her eyes this time. "Thank you, ma'am. I'll be sure to share your compliment with the others. They'll appreciate it, very much. Is there anything I can do for you?"

"No. And, please, continue to put the mail on the desk

each day as you always do. This is my office now. I'll read the mail in here."

Natasha bobbed her head and backed out of the room, closing the door behind her.

Caroline crossed to the desk. She was about to sit, when she thought better of it. Richard's chair was far too big for her and it still smelled of the spicy cologne he favored, the cologne she'd once loved but had grown to hate.

Tomorrow, she'd have one of the maids throw the chair away or give it to charity.

She tried to scoot one of the guest chairs behind the desk instead, but it was too heavy. And pushing it across the plush carpet made her incision hurt. She gave up and plopped down in the guest chair right where it was, on the opposite side of the desk from where Richard must have sat when he was in the office.

The mail contained bills and a few letters from people whose names Caroline didn't recognize, addressed to her.

Surprised someone would send her anything, since she never received any personal mail, she opened the first one. The letter was short but touching, an expression of sympathy from someone who'd worked with her husband. Caroline appreciated the sentiment, even if her own opinion of her husband was a hundred-eighty degrees different than theirs. She'd have to make a point of getting some thank-you notes so she could respond.

The second letter was much shorter than the first. And right to the point. Caroline pressed her hand to her throat as she read it then read it again. She set the note down and opened the drawer where she'd put the papers Leslie had wanted her to sign. When she finished reading them, she was shaking so hard the pages were making rattling noises. She let them flutter to the top of the desk and put her head in her hands.

LUKE STRAIGHTENED IN the driver's seat of his beat-up Thunderbird, parked beneath one of the centuries-old oak trees lining the street next to the Ashton mansion. With Mitch's death so raw and fresh, he wanted nothing more than to drown his grief in a bottle of tequila. But that wouldn't bring Mitch back, and it wouldn't catch whoever had murdered him. Luke figured his best shot at catching the killer was to keep working the Ashton case. Which was why he was sitting outside Caroline's house, instead of getting drunk like he wanted. That and the fact that he was too worried about Caroline's safety to leave. The mansion took up an area the size of an entire city block at the outskirts of Savannah. And there was definitely something strange going on inside. The front door might as well have been a revolving door as often as it had been used since Caroline had gotten home from the funeral.

First to come in was Caroline with her lawyer, Leslie Harrison. After the lawyer left, the place was quiet for another hour. But that was when things got interesting and a bit crazy. Over a dozen men from Stellar Security came in and out of the front door, as if there was some kind of meeting going on inside. That had certainly piqued Luke's interest and had him craving to go up the front steps and knock on the door, in spite of the agreement that he was supposed to hang back. But he waited in the car, taking photos and recording everyone who came and went. Security guard after security guard exited the house until he suspected there weren't any left inside.

Was it possible Caroline had fired them?

Why would she do that? Alex wanted her to keep

everything status quo. Caroline definitely needed protection right now, at least until her husband's killer was caught. If she'd changed her mind and wanted Luke's company to protect her, the problem was that he was the only one available. His other men were all out on assignment.

A bead of sweat slid down the side of his face. Even in the shade it was probably close to ninety degrees. He debated turning the car on to run the air conditioner for a few minutes. But he'd probably feel even hotter once he had to turn it off again.

His phone vibrated on the seat beside him. When he saw who was calling, his gaze shot to the front windows of the mansion. Sure enough, Caroline stood at the glass with a cell phone pressed to her ear, looking right at him.

He picked up the phone. "Is everything okay?"

"No, Luke. Everything is *not* okay."

## Chapter Seven

Caroline had insisted that she and Luke have dinner before she told him whatever it was that had shaken her up so much. He didn't know why she'd insisted on waiting, but he sensed she was near the breaking point and needed a few moments of "normal" in order to cope. That was the only reason he didn't press her. That, and the fact that neither of them had eaten since the funeral, and he figured it would do them both some good.

But the wait was driving him crazy. He needed to *do* something to catch Mitch's killer instead of sitting here doing nothing. His frustration with the delay was compounded when Caroline entered the sunroom at the back of the mansion carrying a tray of sandwiches and drinks. He jumped up from his seat at the small café table and hurried to take the tray from her.

"Shouldn't the cook, or maid, or whoever works for you, bring this in here instead of you carrying it through the house? You were only released from the hospital this morning."

Her face flushed and she took a seat while he set the tray in the middle of the table.

"I suppose you're right," she said. "I hadn't even thought to ask. It will take a while for the staff, and me, to get used to doing things differently now that Richard is gone."

He frowned. "'Differently'?"

"Please, have a sandwich. And some iced tea. I'm sure it must have been horribly hot sitting out in that car."

Her overly bright smile and evasive answer told him far more than she realized, and confirmed what he'd suspected when she'd opened the front door herself and ushered him inside. The staff basically ignored her. Luke couldn't imagine Richard answering his own door. A butler or maid would have done that for him and would have seated the guest, then arranged refreshments.

Rather than embarrass her by pointing out what to him was obvious—that she should fire every last one of the idiots who supposedly worked for her—he quickly finished off a half sandwich and emptied a glass of blessedly cold tea. Caroline ate very little, probably because she was so focused on her manners.

Her back was ramrod straight, her left hand in her lap holding her napkin, which she daintily wiped at the corners of her mouth after every bite, whether she needed to or not. He also noted that she didn't look at him and mostly kept her eyes downcast.

Curious to see what she would do, he propped his elbows on the table. He was pretty sure that was a big no-no according to fancy etiquette rules.

Caroline's gaze flicked toward him, widening, but she quickly looked away. She took another sip of her water, then dabbed at her mouth with the napkin.

Testing her again, he pushed his plate of food away. "That was a delicious dinner, thank you."

Sure enough, she immediately stopped eating, even though her plate was mostly full.

"You're welcome. Is there anything else I can get you?"

He sighed and sat back. "I'd really like to know what got you so spooked. What's going on?"

Her lips pressed together and she stared out the windows at the sparkling pool behind the house. "Do you know how to swim?"

He followed her gaze, not sure where she was going with this. "Yes."

"Is it fun? I always thought it would be. Fun."

"You own a pool and you don't know how to swim?"

She shook her head. "It was Richard's pool, not mine. And, no, I don't know how to swim. My husband always said he was worried I'd burn too easily out in the sun because of my pale complexion." She tapped the arm of her chair. "But that's not the real reason he didn't want me to know how to swim."

"What was the real reason?"

"Fear. Richard liked to invent new ways to control me, to make me afraid. I always figured one day he'd use the pool to teach me one of his lessons. I'm sure he would have, eventually. He just never got around to it."

Luke scooted forward in his chair. "Tell me about these lessons."

She shook her head. "No. That's not something I'm going to share."

"But you *are* sharing, aren't you? You're telling me little bits and pieces of your life, how your husband controlled you and allowed—or perhaps encouraged—the servants to pretty much ignore you from what I've seen."

She bowed her head. "Yes."

"If you don't want to talk about it, why share even some of it?"

Her mouth curved into a harsh smile. "Because I'd hoped that I'd never have to admit the truth to anyone. I'd hoped to keep my shame to myself. Earlier this year, for the first time, I shared a tiny part of what was going on with someone I thought I could trust."

"Your husband's lawyer, Leslie Harrison."

"Yes."

"Did something happen earlier? When she was here?"

She stared at the pool for a moment before answering. "You and Alex were right to doubt her." She rose from her chair. "I'm ready to show you why I called you."

Luke scrambled out of his chair and hurried after her. She led him through the maze that was the mansion, to the front room just off the foyer. He barely had time to realize it was probably her husband's office, when she picked up some papers from the massive desk. She handed an envelope to him.

"Read this first."

The short missive inside was written in carefully printed block letters.

I KNOW YOU KILLED HIM. I KNOW THE WILL IS FAKE. YOU WON'T GET AWAY WITH THIS.

"How did you get this?"

"One of the maids brought it in. From the looks of the envelope, it came through regular mail."

"When?"

"Today, I guess. The maid brought it to me shortly after I got home."

He placed the letter and envelope back on the desk. "We need to call Alex and Detective Cornell."

She laughed bitterly. "Why? So they have more evidence that makes me look guilty?"

"No. So they have more evidence that someone is trying to hurt you, that you're the target."

She grew very still. "What do you mean?"

"I mean that it's most likely the killer sent that note. He's trying to threaten you, scare you. Maybe that's why he killed Mitch. But frightening you isn't his only goal. He wants to torture you, by making you look guilty."

"Well, if that's true, goal accomplished."

He started to round the desk toward her, but she held up her hand. "Wait. That's not all. Leslie tried to get me to sign something earlier today. I thought it was a simple power of attorney, and I told her I wanted to take control of my own affairs now, that I didn't want to give up control to her, but I would think about it. She tried to take the document back, but I put it in the drawer. She was fairly nervous about that. After I received that letter—" she waved toward the note he'd just set down "—I took a fresh look at what she wanted me to sign." She pointed at some papers on another part of the desk.

Luke picked them up, saw the top page was, as she'd said, a typical-looking power-of-attorney form, but then he read the second and third pages. He set the documents down.

"I can see why she was nervous and didn't want you to read the rest. Did she really think you would sign over a huge portion of Ashton Enterprises to her? And make her a voting board member?"

"Apparently so. And the way I've allowed everyone to trample over me for the past few years, I shouldn't be surprised that she thought she could get away with it. Everyone tries to control me or profit off me in some way." Her blue eyes lifted to his. "Except you. You haven't tried to take advantage of me, to push me around. You're the first person who has really listened, and cared enough to look out for my interests. I never would have thought to hire Alex if it weren't for you. And I probably would have signed that paper Leslie gave me if Alex hadn't warned me about being extra careful and holding no one above suspicion."

Tears gathered in her eyes. "And what do you get in return for helping me? Your friend is killed."

Without stopping to think about how she might react, he moved around the desk and gently pulled her toward him, holding her close. At first, she stiffened, but then she melted against him. He reveled in the feel of her softness molded to his hardness and rested his chin against the top of her head.

He told himself he was holding her to make her feel better, but he realized that wasn't the whole truth. Holding her made *him* feel better. For the first time since losing his friend, he felt some of the tightness in his chest begin to ease. He selfishly held her, using her as his lifeline, a balm to his troubled conscience.

"I lost a good friend today," he whispered against her hair. "But I know Mitch wouldn't want either of us to wallow in guilt over his death. He'd want us to work together and find justice."

When she didn't say anything, he pulled back and looked at her. "It's not your fault."

"My brain knows that, but my heart is having a lot harder time with it."

She moved out of his embrace and wrapped her arms around her waist. "What do we do now?"

He resisted the urge to pull her back into his arms, just barely.

"For one thing, I think you should fire Leslie."

Her face paled and her eyes took on a haunted look. "I know. I will. But not today. That's not an easy conversation, especially after she helped me escape Richard. I owe her so much."

"You don't owe her your company, your wealth, and that's what she tried to take. She basically tried to steal it from you, hoping you wouldn't notice."

"You're right. And I will take care of it, just not today."

He didn't like that, but it was her decision to make. "I recommend you don't wait too long. She knows too much about you and your holdings, enough to be dangerous if she can't be trusted, which she's proven she can't." He waved at the letter and the power-of-attorney document. "Are you going to call Alex and Cornell?"

She blinked at him. "You're *asking* me?"

"Of course. I'm not going to try to order you around. You're a full-grown woman." The look of astonishment on her face made him realize what she'd been thinking—that Richard would never have asked her. He would have told her.

Luke stiffened. "Caroline, don't confuse me with your late husband. I would never hurt you, would never try to control you or dictate your actions. Richard Ashton and I are nothing alike."

Her face turned a light shade of pink. "I see that. I'm sorry. I'll try not to confuse the two of you again. Maybe it would make it easier if you'd quit calling me Caroline. That was Richard's preference, not mine. My maiden name was Caroline Bagwell. My friends, my parents, always called me Carol. But Richard thought it sounded too common, so he insisted on calling me Caroline."

Humbled that she would put him in the same category as her friends and family, he smiled. "Carol. It's a beautiful name."

She returned his smile with one of her own. "Thank you." Her smile faded, replaced by a look of worry.

"Is there something else?" he asked. "Something you haven't told me?"

She briefly closed her eyes, and when she opened them, they looked so haunted his heart ached for her.

"After Leslie's visit, and getting that letter in the mail, I searched Richard's desk. I knew he kept his most private papers in those drawers. I guess I just didn't want any more surprises, no more secrets. So I went through all his documents."

She pulled the bottom drawer open, lifted the first piece of paper out and handed it to Luke.

He scanned the short letter, from a private-investigation firm, dated two months earlier. Then he met her tortured gaze and waited.

She sighed and admitted out loud what she already knew. "We need to call Alex and Detective Cornell."

CORNELL FINISHED PUTTING the documents into evidence bags. He sealed them and wrote something across the front in permanent marker before sliding them into his suit-jacket pocket.

Carol sat behind her husband's desk while Alex, Cornell and Luke sat in chairs they'd pulled up to the other side. Carol had to admit Richard was right about one thing: the large desk that dominated the room gave someone a sense of power and control. She decided right then and there that she was going to keep it, and that she would stop thinking of it as Richard's desk. It was her desk now.

"Mrs. Ashton," Cornell said. "That letter from the investigation firm makes it clear your husband suspected Miss Harrison was stealing from him. He was working with that company to entrap her with false documents and information they were feeding her during your weekly visits to her office. It's also clear he was going to fire her soon and provide the evidence he'd gathered to a prosecutor to press charges. Do you have any reason to suspect that Miss Harrison was aware of this, prior to your husband's death?"

She shook her head. "No, I didn't know anything about it until today."

Alex tapped the desk. "Depending on what types of traps the investigator was setting, Miss Harrison may have realized something was 'off' with the documents. She may have been suspicious and figured out what was going on."

"If so," Cornell said, "that gives her motive. I imagine if she lost the Ashton account, she'd be in serious financial trouble. And of course she'd be in danger of losing her license, even if she wasn't found guilty in criminal court. Those are powerful motives for murder." He jotted some notes on his notepad. "What about the anonymous note? Miss Ashton, do you have any reason to believe the will that was filed with the courts was fake as the note states?"

"No. I know my husband drew up a will right after we got married, making me the primary beneficiary. I didn't know the details, of course. And if he changed the will later on, I have no knowledge of it. But Richard wouldn't have told me about it if he had."

He pursed his lips and considered. "It does seem odd that he would only give his family members five million each and give you the rest, with…everything that went on between you two. Seems reasonable that he changed the will later to cut your portion much smaller and give more to his brothers. Do you know if his brothers have much money?"

"They both own their own businesses and live in expensive homes. Not as grand as this one, but certainly not cheap by any means. I'd say they're both doing extremely well without their brother's money."

"Millionaires?"

"I believe so, yes."

"It must have galled them that their brother was a billionaire. Maybe they assumed he'd leave the estate split equally if he died. They would have been shocked when the will was filed and they didn't get much, relatively speaking."

Luke leaned forward in his chair. "You think one of them killed Richard?"

"We've been looking at them all along as potential suspects, but I think we need to dig harder and see what shakes out."

"What about Mitch?" Luke asked. "Have you gotten anywhere with that investigation? Are you convinced his death is related to Ashton's?"

"I'm keeping an open mind on a link, but investigators on both cases are sharing information since it seems highly likely both murders were performed by the same killer. Unfortunately, I don't have anything new to offer you." He turned to Carol. "Have you thought of anyone else who might have wanted to harm your husband?"

"Or harm Caroline," Alex added from his chair on the other side of Cornell. "We haven't established who was the target, her or her husband."

Cornell frowned, obviously not caring for that reminder. "I haven't made up my mind on anything. I'm exploring all possible angles. Mrs. Ashton? Did your husband—or you—have any enemies?"

She shook her head. "Actually, just the opposite. Everyone loved Richard. They thought he was an extraordinary humanitarian." She couldn't help the bitterness that crept into her voice. "I suppose, from the outside looking in, he was. He certainly gave an incredible amount of money each year to charities. As for me, I don't see how I could have made any enemies. I barely know anyone."

"What about your attorney, Leslie Harrison?"

"She's not an enemy right now. I consider her a friend— or I did, until I read that document she left. I imagine the friendship will be over tomorrow, when I fire her. But, honestly, I can't count her as an enemy, at least not as someone who might have wanted to harm either me or my husband."

"It's getting late," Luke said. "I think the more important consideration right now is how to protect Carol."

Alex's brows rose. "'Carol'? Not 'Caroline'?"

"It's what I prefer," she said.

"Carol," Alex corrected himself. "As for protection, I thought there was a team of security guards watching over the mansion, but I didn't see anyone when we drove up."

She cleared her throat. "I fired them—at least, from watching this house. They still handle security for the rest of my husband's—the rest of *my* holdings."

"Any particular reason?" he asked.

She glanced at Luke before responding. "They were my jailers for years. I suppose I wanted to take off my shackles and cast them aside."

Alex's eyes widened, but he didn't say anything else.

"You still need security," Luke said. "Even if nothing was going on, a mansion like this needs a show of security to dissuade would-be thieves. And until we find your husband's killer, you need to assume it's possible the killer was targeting you and therefore you need to be protected."

She looked pointedly at him. "Fine. Then I'd like to hire you instead, permanently, to stand guard over this house."

"While I appreciate the faith, all my guys are still out on other assignments." His mouth tightened. "Not to mention the office is in chaos without Mitch to direct everything."

"I'm sorry for your loss," she said again, offering him a watery smile. "If you need to cancel our contract, I'll understand. But if there is any way for you to keep me as a client and stay here as my personal bodyguard, I'd appreciate it. I can give you money to hire someone to watch the office, and to hire more guards so they can watch the house."

"I'm sure we can work something out, but it will take time. Of course I'll stay to protect you, but I can't do it alone. The house doesn't have a security alarm. And a house this size has dozens of entrance and exit points. Without a full security staff right now, it's not safe."

"Couldn't you get an alarm company to wire the house, like you said you were going to do at the cottage?"

"Yes, but it's after seven o'clock at night, on a Sunday. It will take days to adequately wire this house. That's not something that can be done before tonight. I've got another recommendation. And you're not going to like it."

"What?"

"I think you should rehire Stellar Security, at least until the alarm system is installed and I have a chance to hire some more guards and bring them in."

She bit her bottom lip.

"I agree," Cornell said. "You can't stay here without more guards."

"Then I'll leave. I hate this house anyway. There are no good memories here. I have no intention of living here long-term again. I can go somewhere else."

Alex leaned forward, resting his arms on top of the desk. "The simplest, safest thing for tonight would be to get Stellar Security to send their guards back here. If you don't want to stay, you can plan where to go tomorrow. But tonight, I'd be more worried about you trying to figure out a new place that's safe and arranging all the details. You just don't have enough time for that."

She rubbed her hands up and down her arms. "All right. I'll call Stellar and ask them to guard the house again. But tomorrow I'm moving out."

A LITTLE OVER two hours later, the staff of security guards from Stellar Security was back in place as if they'd never left, with one notable exception—Luke.

Per Caroline's—Carol's—request, he accompanied her everywhere she went. He would have recommended that he stay glued to her side anyway, but having her suggest it made everything smoother, and made him feel good that she trusted him and seemed to derive strength and confidence from his presence.

When she'd spoken to the head of security on the phone, after Alex and Cornell had left, she had tentatively reached for his hand. He took the gesture for what it was. She needed his support, someone to help her find the strength she'd forgotten she had inside her all this time.

But once the security guards arrived, she hadn't needed to hold his hand anymore. He could see her blossoming, coming out of her shell, like a phoenix rising from the ashes. And it amazed him how different she seemed already, less than a week after her husband's influence over her had been severed. Looking at her now, he couldn't imagine she would ever allow another man to control her the way Richard Ashton had. And it made him wonder how she'd gone from the strong woman before him to the timid, insecure woman he'd met that day in his office. Thank God her husband hadn't been able to completely kill the strong woman inside her. Hopefully, in time, she'd learn to smile far more often than she did now and have a happy life. Lord knew she deserved it.

After accompanying him on a tour of the house so he could verify the doors and windows were locked and that there were sufficient guards posted, she led him to the massive winding marble staircase in the two-story foyer. They'd passed it several times today, but she'd never seemed to notice it, as if she was avoiding it. But it couldn't be avoided any longer. It was time for bed. And now, as she paused at the bottom of the staircase and looked up at the next landing, he couldn't miss the telltale shaking of her hands.

He edged closer to her side and did what she'd done earlier: he offered her his hand.

She entwined her fingers with his. "I shouldn't be scared to go up these stairs, but I can't help picturing him up there, waiting, watching, ready to punish me for thinking I could escape him."

"He can't hurt you anymore, unless you let him."

Her mouth tightened. "That's the problem, isn't it? I let him hurt me for so many years. How could I have been so weak, so cowardly, for so long?"

He gently pressed his hand beneath her chin, urging her to look at him. When she did, he leaned down and kissed her forehead. Her eyes widened.

"What was that for?" she whispered.

"A reminder."

"About what?"

"That you're an intelligent, beautiful, strong woman. You faced a monster in this house every day, a man who was over twice your size and used his size to intimidate and hurt you. And in spite of that, you did what few women could have done in your position. You survived. You didn't let him destroy you. Look at what you did today. You made some tough decisions, like deciding to fire someone you had once thought of as a friend, and rehiring the security company because you knew it needed to be done. A coward couldn't have survived what you have and wouldn't be getting stronger every day like you are." He squeezed her hand and gestured toward the second-floor gallery. "Tell me what you see."

Her gaze followed his, up the stairs, pausing on the middle landing, then higher as she looked left and right down the gallery with its doors opening off it.

"I see fear, and misery, and pain," she whispered.

"Do you know what I see up there?"

She shook her head.

"I see a white marble railing. Behind it, I count five wooden doors, with thick, carved molding around them. I see red plaster walls—"

"Burgundy," she said, her voice halting.

"Okay. I see burgundy plaster walls, some little wooden tables with shiny tops."

"Granite tops." Her voice was stronger this time.

"Expensive, pretentious shiny tops." Out of the corner of his eye, he noticed her lips curve into a tiny smile. Encouraged, he continued. "And on the walls of the pretentious gallery are paintings. Most of them are of other buildings or animals, a few portraits here and there. And smack-dab at the top of the stairs is some alleged artist's really blurry, wretched attempt at painting an outdoor scene, but it looks more like a picture taken out of focus."

She let out a burst of laughter. "It's a Monet! And it probably costs more than this entire house."

He cocked his head. "Hmm. Can't say that I see the appeal."

She cocked her head as well, mimicking him. "Honestly, I don't see its appeal, either." Her eyes danced with laughter as she smiled up at him.

Unable to resist the impulse, he brushed her hair back from her forehead.

Her smile faded, but she didn't look upset that he'd been so familiar. Instead, she looked puzzled.

"I should be afraid of you," she said.

He stiffened. "I would never, ever hurt you."

"I know. I'm not sure how I know, but I know. You're a large, muscular, incredibly handsome man."

He grinned. "Good to know."

"That wasn't a compliment. Big men, handsome men, scare me. Normally. Because I expect them to be like my husband. But you're…different. You make me smile. And you make me feel…safe."

She turned back toward the stairs. Her eyes were still full of shadows, but she squared her shoulders, and her mouth tightened into a determined line. "Let's do this."

THE HOUSE WAS DARK, silent. The live-in staff had retreated to the wing on the opposite side of the estate hours ago. And Carol was asleep in the guest room next to Luke's. So what had woken him?

He slid out of bed, yanked his jeans on and shoved his gun into the back of his waistband. Moving as quietly as possible, he rushed through the open doorway that joined his room with Carol's. She was lying in the middle of the bed, looking like a fairy princess in her diaphanous, long, white nightgown, her golden hair splayed out on the pillow around her like a halo. The door from her bedroom to the hallway was still locked. If he'd heard something in his sleep, it hadn't come from this room.

He hurried back to his own room and eased the door to the hall open. Wall sconces along the gallery spaced about every twenty feet gave off a dim glow, like expensive, crystalline night-lights. Just enough light to change the pitch black to a muddy gray, to reveal images, shapes, but little else. Enough light to keep someone from stubbing their toe on one of the decorative tables that lined the hallway, or to keep them from stumbling against the marble balustrade and taking a nasty fall to the foyer two stories below.

He waited, listening intently, watching. But he didn't see or hear anything. He thought about going downstairs to check on the guards, but that would mean leaving Carol upstairs alone. Not an option. Instead, he pocketed the door key to his room and locked the door closed behind him to prevent anyone from going inside and getting to her that way. He quietly made his way to the end of the gallery, listening at each door, then quickly searching each room until he stood in front of the double doors that led to the one room he hadn't searched. The master bedroom.

Earlier, when Carol had led him upstairs and pointed out the guest rooms where they would both stay, she'd waved toward the end of the hall and announced that was the master bedroom. But she hadn't looked at it, and she'd quickly turned and gone into her own room after saying good-night.

Now he stood in front of the elaborately carved double doors, carefully turned the knob, then eased one of the doors open. The room was surprisingly well lit, as if the former occupants didn't like the dark. Dim light filtered from wall sconces spaced throughout the room, much like the ones in the gallery.

He edged farther inside. Everything was neat, nothing out of place. The four-poster bed in the center dominated the expansive room. He didn't think he'd ever seen a bed that large and imposing. The man who slept in a bed like that had to feel as if he was king of the world. And the woman who had slept there had to have felt as if she was…lost.

He forced thoughts of Carol away. He needed to focus, search the room. Then get back to his own. He moved into the adjoining bathroom, with its sunken tub and walk-in, glassless shower. He'd always considered his own master bathroom to be rather large, but he could have fit two of them in here.

He headed back into the bedroom and stopped. Something was off. Out of the corner of his eye, he realized a door that had been closed when he entered the room was now open. He clawed for his gun but he was too late. A dark shape launched itself from the closet. Luke twisted, slamming his shoulder into his attacker's sternum.

The man grunted with pain and staggered back, knocking over a delicate decorative table. A vase on the table fell to the marble floor and crashed, sending shards of glass flying across the room, pinging against the walls.

Luke lunged forward, but before he could throw a punch, his prey scrambled out of the way and took off in a dead run for the double doors. Luke ran after him, drawing his gun as he dashed through the open doorway onto the gallery.

"Hold it. Freeze or I'll shoot," Luke yelled.

The man skidded to a stop and slowly raised his hands. As he turned around, the door to Carol's room opened. She faced Luke, not seeing the intruder. She stepped into the hallway.

"Get back in your room," he shouted as he raced toward her. He couldn't shoot with her between him and the intruder.

The seconds seemed to drag by as everything happened at once.

Carol turned around.

The intruder grabbed her and yanked her in front of him. The glint of a knife winked in the light from one of the hall sconces. He held it to her throat.

Luke skidded to a stop just a few feet away.

The man had one hand manacled around Carol's waist, the other holding the knife at her throat. He crouched down behind her so Luke couldn't get a clear shot at him. His face was covered with a ski mask. He slowly backed toward the stairs, pulling Carol with him.

"Let her go," Luke demanded.

Carol whimpered and clutched the arm at her throat.

"There's no way I'm letting you out of this house with her," Luke said. "And there's no way you can get down the stairs without me getting a clear shot at you at some point. Your only hope is to let her go."

The man stopped. "If I let her go," he rasped, his voice sounding oddly forced, strained, "you'll just shoot me."

*In a heartbeat.* The man had signed his death warrant the second he held a knife to Carol's throat.

"Not if you don't hurt her," Luke lied.

The man backed a few more steps down the hall.

Luke followed relentlessly, his gun out in front of him.

Suddenly the man backed up against the baluster. "Drop the gun or I toss her over."

The blood drained from Luke's face. He hesitated.

The man lifted Carol a few inches off the floor.

She gasped, her eyes rolling white with fear.

"All right, all right. Don't hurt her." Luke knelt down and placed his gun on the floor.

"Kick the gun away from you," the man ordered.

Luke kicked it behind him, away from the intruder.

"Now back up."

He weighed his options.

The intruder lifted Carol higher.

Luke swore and backed up several feet.

The man lowered the knife from Carol's throat and peered at Luke over her shoulder. The face-off by the baluster seemed to stretch out forever, but only a few seconds had really gone by when the intruder heaved Carol up over the banister.

She screamed as he slapped her hands around the top of the railing and let go, leaving her hanging on all by herself, her feet dangling over the two-story drop, as he raced for the stairs.

## Chapter Eight

Luke charged forward as the intruder raced away from him. The man had been smart, forcing Luke to make a choice between catching him and helping Carol.

There *was* no choice.

Luke lunged for the railing and leaned over, grabbing Carol beneath the arms and hauling her up and over. He fell back with her to the gallery floor, holding her in his arms. She buried her face against his chest, shaking uncontrollably, tears hot and wet against his skin.

Below them, the assailant raced across the foyer and out the front door, disappearing into the night.

LUKE CROUCHED DOWN in front of the couch where Carol was sitting, wrapped in a heavy terry-cloth robe, her face almost as white as the wall behind her.

"Are you sure I can't get you something? Aspirin? A drink?"

She shook her head but didn't say anything.

He sighed heavily and sat beside her. "I can call a doctor. Maybe you'd like something stronger, to take off the edge. Something to help you sleep."

She shook her head more forcefully this time. "No. No drugs. I don't want to go to sleep. Not here." Her eyes turned pleading. "Please," she whispered, "take me somewhere else. Anywhere. Somewhere safe."

His heart felt as if it was breaking as he looked at her mournful face. "I will. In a few minutes, okay?"

"Okay." She sank back against the cushions.

The house blazed with light now and was full of security guards and police officers, as well as the cook and two of the maids. They were the only live-in servants and had been roused from their rooms on the other side of the mansion by Cornell and his men. But they hadn't seen or heard anything that might help with the investigation. So, now they were busily laying out an assortment of refreshments for their unexpected visitors.

Cornell spoke in the corner of the family room to the guards' supervisor, who looked angry enough to kill someone. He'd already lambasted the entire staff for allowing the intruder inside, but now that they knew how the intruder had gotten in, Luke almost felt sorry for the guards. Almost.

The intruder had ambushed the guard at the front door and left him bound and gagged in the bushes, hog-tied with no hope of getting himself freed. He'd done the same thing to two other guards, leaving the front totally clear for him to sneak on in. Which just proved Luke's original theory, that the mansion required a security alarm, a high-tech one that was tamper-proof, or as close as possible to one.

When Cornell finished with the supervisor, he hurried to Luke. He glanced uncertainly at Carol, before motioning for Luke to step away with him.

As soon as Luke started to get up from the couch, Carol started to get up to follow him. He glanced at Cornell, shook his head, then sat back down.

"You might as well say whatever you need to say in front of her," Luke said.

Cornell dragged the coffee table closer and sat on it facing them. "Okay, here's where we stand. Other than your basic description of a white man, at least six feet tall, a hundred ninety pounds, wearing dark clothes, I've got nothing to go on. And since the grass out front is so thick, I don't even have a shoe print. I need another angle to figure out who this guy is. What I need to know is why he was here." He looked at Carol. "Mrs. Ashton, it seems likely the intruder was after you, since he went to the master bedroom. But if he was going to kill you, he could have just tossed you over the banister instead of making sure you were clutching the top rail before he took off."

"Or he knew if he hurt her I'd kill him," Luke said. "He may have been trying to kill her but had to change his plan to make sure he survived the night."

"If that's the case, then perhaps he went into the master bedroom looking for something besides Mrs. Ashton. Can we go up there together? See if something is missing?"

"All right," she said, her voice soft but steady.

She moved like a wraith through the living room, but this time she didn't cling to Luke's hand. She walked with dignity, somehow having pulled herself together for the task at hand. Cornell and Luke followed her up the staircase and down the long hall to the bedroom. Everything was quiet, like a church, until she pulled the doors open. Then the steady buzz of crime-scene investigators talking as they dusted for prints and searched for forensic evidence assaulted them.

Luke exchanged a startled look with Cornell.

Carol must have noticed the look, because she half

turned. "The room is soundproof," she said. Her mouth twisted bitterly. "So no one would hear my screams."

She went inside, leaving Luke and Cornell shaken and staring after her.

"I wish that bastard was still alive so I could kill him," Luke said.

Cornell's mouth lifted in a half smile. "Honestly, I'd probably be right there with you. The guy really was a class-A bastard."

They entered the suite and stood back, watching Carol slowly make her way around the room, weaving among the investigators as they collected evidence.

She seemed to wander in no particular pattern, stopping to open a drawer, or a jewelry box, or one of the three closet doors. Luke watched her closely, a suspicion growing inside him. If anything, her search was almost too random, as if she was trying to make sure no one paid her any particular attention or realized she was looking for something specific.

"I'm going to chat with the team lead and see if they've found anything," Cornell said.

Luke nodded but didn't take his gaze off Carol.

When she turned toward him, he looked off to the side, pretending interest in the tech nearest to him, dusting the top of a chest of drawers. A few seconds later, Luke looked back toward her. She opened a drawer in another chest and reached her hand all the way in. She felt around, then her eyes widened, and she felt around again. Whatever she was searching for obviously wasn't there.

She briefly shut her eyes as if in pain, then closed the drawer.

Luke averted his gaze.

Carol crossed the room and stood beside him.

"Anything missing?" he asked.

She wrapped her arms around her waist and shook her head. "No. I'm going back to the guest room to lie down for a few minutes."

Disappointment flashed through him that she didn't feel she could confide in him. "Hang on a second." He waved one of the security guards positioned at the doorway over to him. He read the tag on his shirt and addressed him by name. "Mrs. Ashton is going to lie down. Go with her and stand guard outside the door."

"Yes, sir."

Carol glanced uncertainly at Luke, obviously confused that he wasn't the one who was going to watch over her.

"I'll be there in a couple of minutes," he said. "I need to ask Cornell a few questions."

Some of the worry went out of her, but she still didn't look happy about trusting her care to one of the security guards.

Luke's supposed questions for Cornell were just a ruse to get Carol to leave. He waited until she was out of the room and he heard the guest-bedroom door close down the hall before hurrying to the chest of drawers she'd been so interested in. He pulled the same drawer open that she had opened earlier and reached inside. The drawer was empty, which struck him as odd since the rest of the chest contained clothes. But what would have been at the back of the drawer that she'd been searching for?

He felt all four corners, then pressed against the back of it. Still nothing. Then he turned his hand palm up and felt along the top. His fingers brushed against cold metal and a tiny cord. What the heck?

He straightened, pulled the entire drawer out of the chest and set it on top of the bed. The drawer was empty, but he'd expected that. The metallic object was attached to the chest itself, above the drawer.

Cornell crossed the room, his brow furrowed. "You find something?"

"Maybe. Give me a hand?"

Together, they lifted the chest and moved it about a foot away from the wall.

"That's enough," Luke said.

They set it down and bent to examine the back of the dresser. The little cord Luke had seen came out a hole in the back and went into the wall.

Cornell raised a brow. "What is that?"

"Got a flashlight?"

"Always." The detective pulled a penlight out of his suit-jacket pocket and handed it to Luke.

Luke shined the light into the cavity now exposed without the drawer covering it. He reached in and un-clicked the object he'd found and pulled it out.

"Is that what I think it is?" Cornell asked.

"If you're thinking it's a camera, yeah. It is." Luke examined it. "Looks like it's motion activated."

They both glanced at the bed, which was where the camera had been pointed. There must have been a small gap above the drawer that gave the camera a clear view to the bed.

"Sick jerk," Luke swore.

"You won't find an argument here."

Luke pressed the side of the little camera and opened it. "Looks like there was a video card in here, but it's gone."

"I can't imagine the intruder broke in to get his jollies watching videos of a married couple in their bed."

"Me neither. I think he was after something else."

"I'll tell the techs to be on the lookout for a video card. Maybe Mr. Ashton had put it somewhere else and the camera was empty." He shook his head. "These cases get stranger and stranger the older I get."

"If there was one camera, there may be more," Luke said.

"Understood." Cornell headed to one of the techs.

Luke set the camera on top of the chest of drawers. The more he learned about Richard Ashton, the more he despised the man. He would have liked to believe the camera really was empty, that Ashton hadn't used it to record whatever he did with Carol in this room. But Luke was willing to bet that wasn't the case.

The real question was—who else knew about that video card? Did the intruder know? Had he removed the card after getting whatever it was he wanted from the bedroom so no one would have the video of him?

To answer that, he needed to confront Carol. And that was not a confrontation he was looking forward to.

A LIGHT KNOCK sounded on the guest-room door. Carol drew the quilt up to her chest.

"Who is it?"

"Luke. Can I come in?"

She sat up and scooted against the headboard. "Come in."

He stepped inside, shut and locked the door behind him. Normally she'd have thought he was being a little overcautious, locking the door when there were dozens of police officers and security guards right outside. But after tonight, she wasn't sure there was any such thing as being "too careful."

He perched on the edge of the bed, one leg on the floor, the other bent at the knee resting on top of the mattress.

"I know about the camera."

She sucked in a breath.

"Sorry. I shouldn't have been so blunt."

"No, no, that's okay," she said. "That's one of the reasons I trust you. You're honest, straightforward. I know what to expect around you. And believe me, that means a lot." She shoved her hair out of her face, belatedly wishing she'd taken the time to brush it or braid it. "Now you know one of my secrets. My husband liked to film everything that went on in the bedroom."

He reached out his hand, palm up, and waited.

That was something else she liked about him. He didn't grab for her hand or try to do anything she didn't want to do. He was patient, calm, and let her make the choice. And he seemed to understand how much she craved human contact, no matter how small, after so many years of only being touched by a monster.

She blinked back unexpected tears and threaded her fingers with his.

"You wanted to get the video card when you went into the bedroom," he said. "Did you find it? Did you bring it in here and hide it somewhere?"

"No. I didn't. Yes, I looked for it. I had forgotten about it earlier. The camera has been there so long, I quit paying attention to it years ago. But when I saw everyone in the bedroom, I remembered. I didn't want my shame to end up as fodder for the police in their squad room, or worse, to end up on some internet site for everyone to see."

"Your shame?"

She glanced longingly toward the door.

"Carol, you don't have to tell me anything you don't want to. But if there's anything at all that you can think of that might explain why someone would break into the house and go into the master bedroom, let me know."

"The only thing I saw that was missing was the video card. So…I have to think that was the reason for the break-in. But other than showing…how Richard…hurt me, there wouldn't be any point in taking the card. What value would that be to anyone?"

He stared at her for a long moment, his mouth tightening. "I wish I could take away the hurt, roll back time somehow and spare you from whatever he did to you."

She lifted his hand and kissed the back of it. "Thank you. You really seem to care. I don't know why you do, but I… It means the world to me. It's been so long since anyone…cared."

"I want to hold you, Carol. Will you let me hold you?"

His request startled her so much she dropped his hand.

He winced. "I guess not. Sorry. I thought—"

She put her hand on his again. "I would like that very much."

He raked the covers down and slid underneath them, fully dressed. He put his arm around her waist and pulled her close, her back to his chest.

"I told you earlier I'd take you somewhere else tonight, but it's only a few more hours until dawn. There's a security guard right outside the door. And once the police leave, there will still be a dozen guards throughout the house, working in pairs this time. If you're okay with waiting, we can both rest for a little while and figure out a new plan in the morning. Are you okay with that? Staying here until morning?"

In answer, she snuggled into the pillow, content to have his arm around her. With Richard, the arm would have felt like an anchor, pulling her under, drowning her.

But with Luke, it was a protective circle, making her feel safe, cherished, as if—for once—she actually mattered.

As soon as Carol woke the next morning, she took care of a task that she'd been dreading, but that she knew had to be done for her to move forward. She called Leslie and fired her. Leslie hadn't taken the news well, and the call had turned ugly.

After that, Carol had straightened her shoulders and informed Luke she was going to pack and leave. Her destination? Anywhere but the house where she'd lived for the past five years. No, correction—she'd told Luke four-and-a-half years. For the first six months of her marriage she and Richard had lived in a smaller house about an hour outside of Savannah.

Which was where they were going right now.

Luke was still shocked she wanted to go to a home she'd shared with her late husband, but while driving there in his beat-up old Thunderbird—which he'd insisted on taking rather than her car since hers had a GPS tracker on it—she'd told him a lot more about her past. She'd explained how she'd met Richard when she was a struggling waitress. He'd taken her from a life of poverty to a life she never could have imagined.

That first six months, Carol had explained, had been pure bliss. They'd been happy, until their first fight. It was over something silly, something she couldn't even remember now. It wasn't the argument that stuck in her mind. It was Richard's reaction to the argument. He'd been absolutely livid that she disagreed with him. His eyes had darkened to almost black. His face had turned a bright red. And then, so quickly she didn't have time to even comprehend what he was going to do, he'd slammed his fist into her jaw.

He'd seemed just as horrified as she was after he hit her, but everything changed that day. At first she'd been too shocked, and too busy nursing her bruised jaw, to even contemplate leaving him. And then he'd spent the next two weeks doing everything he could to make it up to her. He'd apologized over and over, waited on her every need and sworn he would never, ever hurt her again. She'd believed him, even if she was a bit wary.

But the honeymoon was officially over, and the magic of their lovers' hideaway was destroyed. Both of them knew it, even if they didn't admit it. Richard purchased the mansion in town and they moved. They'd never returned to their hideaway. But he hadn't sold the house. He had a service come in once a week to clean it, and stock it, just in case they ever wanted to go there on vacation or for the weekend. But they never had. Which was why Carol was certain no one would ever think to look for her there.

Luke parked his car under a tree a short distance from the house, where it wouldn't be easily noticed from the road. He hadn't been keen on the idea of going to one of Richard's holdings, but the place did look deserted and they hadn't passed anyone on the two-lane road for the last half hour. They certainly couldn't have gone to *his* house since he was in the phone book. And it wasn't exactly a secret that he was her bodyguard. Maybe this would work out.

He went around to the other side of the car to open the door, but Carol didn't wait. She opened it herself and met him at the trunk. He popped the trunk open and grabbed their bags, which only had a few days' worth of clothes. He'd had her ditch her larger bag back at the mansion and pack a smaller one with a shoulder strap like his to keep his hands free.

He kept an eye on the road as they hurried up the walkway to the two-story house that, although nowhere near as big as the mansion in Savannah, was still considerably larger than average.

Carol punched a code into the electronic keypad to unlock the door.

"That's unusual," Luke said.

"Maybe for most people, but not for Richard. He insisted on keypads instead of physical keys for properties he rarely visited. It made it easier for him to be spontaneous without having to worry about finding the property manager to get the keys."

"From what I've read of him in the papers, he didn't strike me as the spontaneous type."

She hesitated. "He wasn't always the man you read about in the papers. But you're right. At least for the bulk of our marriage, he wasn't spontaneous. He was much more…controlled."

Luke immediately regretted saying anything about her husband. Yes, she'd brought him up first, but it was Luke's comment that put that spark of hurt, that flash of fear, back in her eyes. He sensed there were many more layers of pain inside her, and every once in a while one of those layers would reveal itself. He just hoped she'd be able to talk it all out someday, and then maybe she'd start feeling whole again. Richard had hurt her so much in life. Luke hated that the man had the power to continue to hurt her in death.

She led the way inside the foyer to the two-story family room in the middle of the house. It was surprisingly dust free, but then again, if a property-management company was coming in once a week to clean the place, it made sense. Especially with no one living there to make any messes.

"Let's check the kitchen," Carol said. "If the manager keeps it stocked with fresh groceries like he's supposed to, I might be able to whip us up something for breakfast. That is, if I can remember what I used to know about cooking."

She started forward, but he stepped in front of her.

"I need to search the house first, make sure there aren't any unwelcome visitors hanging around."

Her mouth tightened at the reminder that they might not be safe, but she didn't argue.

"This place is too big for a quick search. You'll need to come with me so I'm not worried leaving you down here by yourself, okay?"

"I wasn't looking forward to being left alone, so that's fine with me."

He gave her the keys to his car and pulled out his gun. "If anything happens to me, I want you to promise you'll run. Get out of here. Don't try to help me and don't stop for anyone until you're in a public area surrounded by other people. Promise?"

Her back stiffened. "I'm not going to be a coward and run away. I can help. If nothing else, I can knock someone over the head with a lamp or something."

"No way. I don't want to risk your getting hurt." From the mutinous look that flashed across her face, he knew she wasn't going to do as he said. He decided to go for her main weakness—her soft heart. "Let me put that another way. If you're in the way, or if I have to worry about you while I'm trying to fight for my life, the distraction could get me hurt or killed."

She crossed her arms. "You're just saying that to make me feel guilty."

"Is it working?"

She rolled her eyes. "Yes. Fine, I won't get in the way. I'll go for help."

"Thank you." He waited, trying not to laugh, knowing her impeccable manners wouldn't allow that comment to stand on its own.

"You're welcome," she said between clenched teeth.

He waited until he turned around to smile. "Let's check upstairs first."

Had he really thought this house was smaller than the one in town? From the front, it appeared smaller. But there seemed to be just as many doors upstairs as at the other house, with just as many places to hide. The only good thing was that there wasn't an open banister across the upstairs hallway where someone could be thrown over. He forced the unpleasant reminder of Carol's near miss out of his mind and continued the search through the bedrooms and bathrooms.

Carol followed along, her fingers occasionally tracing some small object, as if reliving a memory. A good memory, from the dreamy, faraway look in her eyes. That should have made Luke happy, to know that she had some good memories from the early part of her marriage—heaven knew, she deserved and needed some good memories—but he wasn't nearly as selfless as she was. And he was okay admitting, to himself at least, that he was jealous of those early memories.

When he was satisfied no one was lying in wait for them upstairs, they headed down the second staircase, at the end of the hall, that led directly into the kitchen downstairs. They made a complete circuit of the first floor and ended up back in the foyer.

"Satisfied?" She set the keys he'd given her on the half wall by the door.

"Satisfied."

"Then let's eat. I'm starving." She led the way through the family room to the adjoining kitchen and went straight for the refrigerator.

"Remind me to send a thank-you note to the property manager once this is all over," she said. "He's definitely keeping the place clean and stocked with groceries. We have fresh milk and eggs and everything I need to make omelets. Do you like omelets?"

"Sure. I could just eat cereal, though. No one has to go to the trouble of cooking. And you sure don't need to wait on me." He located what appeared to be the pantry, next to the refrigerator, and opened the door to look for some cereal.

Carol's soft hand on his stopped him.

"I know I don't *have* to cook for you. That's why I want to. Okay?"

He saw the truth in her eyes, so he closed the pantry door. "How can I help?"

"Just sit down at the island and stay out of my way."

He laughed. "I'm starting to like this new Carol, Commander Carol," he teased.

"Commander Carol. Hmm. I could get used to that."

She hummed a low tune as she cut up some peppers and ham then whisked the ingredients together in a pan over the gas stove top.

As she cooked their breakfast, Luke set a pot of coffee brewing and poured them some orange juice. He was used to eating his meals off paper plates and using disposable forks and cups, but he figured she was used to an entirely different style of living, so he rummaged through the cabinets and drawers and set the table the way his mother had taught him years ago.

Carol slid a perfect-looking omelet onto his plate and

a smaller version onto hers. "I probably would have used paper plates and plastic forks, myself. Less to clean later."

He laughed. "Me, too. I just figured…"

She straightened, her smile disappearing. "That I was a snob?"

"No, not at all. I figured you were used to…better. That's all."

She put the pan in the sink and sat on the barstool across from him. "Sorry. I'm being overly sensitive. It's just that…I played a role for so long, pretending to be someone I wasn't. I'm only just now beginning to remember the real me again."

They ate in silence, but it was a comfortable silence. When they were done, they both cleaned the kitchen. Luke wiped his hands on a paper towel and tossed it in the garbage.

"That was the best omelet I've had in ages," he said.

She grinned. "I'm surprised they came out so well. It's been ages since I last cooked."

"When?"

"At a diner, a few hours west of here, in a tiny town called Chester. That's where I lived…before, with my parents."

He shook his head. "Don't think I've heard of Chester."

"Not many people have. It's basically a blip on State Road 126, in Dodge County. Most of the few hundred people who live there commute to work in bigger towns or they work on farms."

"What did you and your parents do?"

"They were short-order cooks at a diner. I was a waitress most of the time, but my father taught me to cook when things were slow."

"You met Richard there," he said, urging her to continue.

"Yes. He was traveling on business, back when he used

to drive himself places, before his businesses exploded into the stratosphere and he went from well-off to rich beyond imagination. I was nineteen. He was twenty-nine, handsome, funny. The first time he came into the diner, he was lost. I gave him directions. The next time he came in specifically to see me. Less than a year later we were married. And for a little while, he really was my white knight." Her lips twisted. "Who am I kidding? He was never a white knight. He didn't change after he married me. He was already the man he would always be. He just hid it well and I was too blinded by his money and his handsome face to see past the facade."

She crossed her arms and leaned back against the sink. "Maybe coming here was a mistake. I'm surrounded by memories, wallowing in the past. Did my husband and I have some good times? Yes. We did. Most of them in this house. But that ended a long time ago. I'll never understand why he treated me the way he did, or why I took it for so long, but the only way I'm ever going to move forward is to truly put my past behind me. And I can't do that until my husband's killer, until Mitch's killer, is caught, and I can begin a new life—not a life of hiding out in the country, either."

He winced at the reference to Mitch. He hadn't allowed himself to grieve for his friend, not yet. He needed to keep his emotions locked away so he could focus on his primary duty: keeping Carol safe.

He pushed himself away from the sink and faced her. "What are you saying?"

"I'm saying I'd like to leave. Let's go somewhere else, somewhere without my husband's ghost hanging over us. And once we're there, I want to call Detective Cornell and Alex Buchanan and find out what's going on with the investigation. I'm a wealthy woman, Luke. I can hire any number of private investigators. I've been sleepwalking and cowering through this entire ordeal instead of thinking for myself. Not anymore. I'm going to throw all my resources into catching this killer so I don't have to hide and cower ever again."

"Sounds good to me. We'll figure out another place to stay once we're on the highway."

They headed through the family room again and into the foyer. Luke picked up their bags and settled the straps over his shoulders. He was about to open the front door, when he glanced at the half wall where she'd left the keys earlier.

The keys weren't there.

"Carol, run!" He let the bags drop to the floor and whirled around.

Something hard slammed against the side of his head. White-hot agony spiked through his skull. Carol's screams echoed through the room as Luke dropped to his knees.

## Chapter Nine

"Run, run, run!" Luke yelled as he wrestled with the man who'd walloped him with the baseball bat in the foyer.

Carol took off as fast as she could through the family room. Leaving Luke behind was one of the hardest things she'd ever done, but she remembered what he'd told her about being a distraction. He'd made her promise that if something like this happened, she wouldn't try to help him—she'd try to escape instead.

She zipped into the kitchen and raced up the back staircase to the second floor. The sounds of fighting continued behind her, which gave her hope that Luke might be okay if he was able to continue to wrestle with the man who'd attacked him—the man with a ski mask on, the same man who'd been in the house in Savannah last night, and most likely the man who'd killed Richard and Mitch. But how had he known she would come to this house? And why did he want to kill her, too?

She prayed that she and Luke would survive long enough to get the answers to those questions.

*Bam!* A gunshot echoed through the house. Carol froze in the middle of the upstairs hallway. Where had the shot come from? Behind her in the kitchen? Or ahead of her down the main staircase? She waited, being as still and quiet as she could while she listened for another sound to tell her who had fired that shot and where they were. But no more sounds came from belowstairs.

She inched her way down the dark hallway. With all the doors closed upstairs, the only sunlight that filtered in was from the staircases, leaving the long hall almost pitch-black. She could turn on the lights but she didn't dare. Instead, she tiptoed down the wooden floors toward the front of the house to peek down into the foyer.

When she reached the stairs, she flattened herself against the wall and carefully leaned around the corner.

A hand clamped over her mouth. Another hand yanked her backward against a hard, warm body. She bit down on the finger pressed against her lips.

Her attacker jerked against her but didn't remove his hand. Instead, he cupped it so she couldn't bite him again. He pulled her back, away from the stairs in spite of her struggles and into one of the bedrooms. He eased the door shut behind them.

He spun her around, moving his hand to keep it over her mouth as his other hand now cupped the back of her head so she couldn't get away. She looked up into a pair of chocolate-brown eyes and slumped in relief. Luke.

She pulled his hand away from her mouth, wincing when she saw the clear impression of her teeth on his skin. "I'm sorry," she whispered, but he was already crossing to the window.

He pulled the heavy draperies back and looked down.

Carol rushed to him. "There aren't any balconies on this house," she said, keeping her voice low. "And a brick porch extends the entire length of the back. There's no way out through these windows."

He dropped the curtain back into place. "What about the front windows?"

She shook her head. "Pretty much the same. If we're

lucky, we might drop onto one of the shrubs, but they're not exactly soft, either." She frowned and feathered her hand across the side of his head, where his dark hair was matted with blood.

He ducked away and hurried to the door.

"You need stitches," she said. "Do you have double vision? Are you hurt anywhere else? I heard a gunshot, but I—"

He held one finger to his lips, signaling her to be quiet.

She nodded, letting him know she understood.

He opened the door and peered into the hallway.

A knife suddenly glinted in front of Carol's face as a hand wrapped around her from behind, holding the knife at her throat. She sucked in a breath.

Luke jerked around, his brows lowering in a thunder-cloud when he saw the man holding Carol.

"How did you get in here?" Luke demanded.

"That doesn't matter," the man rasped in Carol's ear, his voice oddly distorted as if he was purposely trying to change it. "What matters is that I've got her. And I'm not letting her go until I get what I want."

Luke took a step toward them, but stopped and put up his hands when the knife bit into Carol's throat.

"Ease up," he said. "Don't hurt her."

"If you don't want her hurt, then keep your distance."

Luke straightened and adopted a bored look. "What do you want?"

"I want her to admit what she's done."

"I haven't done any—"

"Shut up." He jerked her hair.

She gasped and strained against him, trying to ease the pressure on her scalp.

"You're a murderer," he said in his thick rasp. "I know you had Richard killed. The only question is—who's your accomplice? Who's the one who actually shot the gun so you wouldn't have to dirty your own hands?"

"That other door over there," Luke said, waving a hand toward the door at the back-right corner of the room. "That leads to a bathroom, right? A bathroom that leads to an adjoining bedroom? That's how you got in here."

"Yeah, so? What does it matter?"

"It matters a lot. It tells me you know this house just as well as Carol does. And it explains how you knew the security code to get in the front door. The only question is—which brother are you? Daniel or Grant?"

Carol gasped.

The man behind her swore and pulled his hand away from her throat. He shoved her toward Luke. She stumbled forward. Luke grabbed her and pushed her behind him, blocking her with his body as he faced the other man. Luke slowly backed up, pushing her along with him.

The man standing on the other side of the room wasn't holding the knife anymore. He must have tucked it into his clothing somewhere. But in its place was a gun—Luke's gun. He must have gotten it away from him in the struggle downstairs.

"You seemed tougher at the hospital," Luke said, still backing up, "when you weren't sucker punching anyone with a baseball bat or holding a gun on them. Why don't you put the gun away, take off your mask and face me like a man, Grant."

The man cursed again. He yanked the ski mask off. Sure enough, Grant stared back at both of them, his face mottled red and furious. But he didn't lower the gun.

"How did you know?" he demanded.

"It was a guess. I figured I had a fifty-fifty chance of being right." Luke stiffened and looked off to his right, toward the open bathroom door. "What the hell is he doing here?"

Grant jerked around toward the bathroom.

Luke yanked the bedroom door open and lunged through the doorway into the hall, pulling Carol with him.

An angry shout told them Grant wasn't too far behind. He'd fallen for Luke's distraction but not for long.

"In here." Luke opened a door and shoved Carol inside. But instead of following her, he closed the door, cocooning her in the darkness of the hall closet.

Carol froze at the sound of his footsteps pounding on the wooden floor of the hallway. She squeezed her hands so hard the nails bit into her palms. Why hadn't he come with her? She knew the answer. He was making himself the target, giving her a chance to get away.

A shout sounded down the hallway. A shot rang out, sounding impossibly loud in the narrow confines of the closet. More footsteps pounded against the floor, running past the closet. What was happening? Was Luke okay? Was he hurt, shot, bleeding?

The image of her late husband lying dead on the kitchen floor of the cottage filled her mind. But instead of *his* face, she saw *Luke's* face, cold and pale.

No! She had to help him. She twisted the doorknob, determined to find Luke. But she hesitated. He'd been emphatic about her not trying to help him if something happened. He'd made her promise to escape if at all possible, to go for help. It wasn't as if she could just call the police. Her cell phone was in her purse, which was downstairs in her overnight bag. Luke had his phone, or at least she thought he did. But would he get a chance to use it? Or had it broken during the struggle with Grant in the foyer?

What were her options? Driving Luke's car was out. She didn't have the keys. But Richard kept a car out back in the garage in case he ever visited the house. The keys would be in the garage, too, hanging in the cabinet with the same code to unlock it that was used for the front door. If she could make it out of the house without being seen, she could drive to town and get help.

The image of Luke lying on the floor, bleeding, flashed through her mind again. All her adult life she'd made the wrong choices. She'd chosen the wrong man. She'd believed he was sorry every time he hurt her and she kept giving him chance after chance to change, until everything went so far she was too scared to even try to leave. And now here she was, faced with another choice. If she did what Luke had asked, she might be able to get help. But the nearest town was thirty minutes away. Round trip that was an hour, plus the time to find help, and the time to run to the garage and sneak out the car. If Luke was hurt, could he last an hour, or longer?

She squared her shoulders. That wasn't a chance she was willing to take. She knew this house. Every inch of it. She knew all its secrets, every connected room, every little alcove or storage place. There were panels in some of the walls both upstairs and down that no one would know about if they hadn't been shown. She could well imagine Richard giving Grant the code to get into the house in case he ever wanted to get away or use the house for vacation. But there was no way Richard would share all the little secrets the house contained. Which meant she had an advantage over Grant.

As she inched the door open, the uncertainty and fear she'd felt earlier were, amazingly, gone. She'd made her decision. And for once, she knew it was the *right* decision. If she died today, she would die as a strong, brave woman who was willing to risk everything to save a good man. That was far better than living the rest of her life wondering if she could have done something to help Luke.

She poked her head out the door and looked up and down the dimly lit hallway. She listened intently, searching the shadows, but no sounds alerted her to anyone close by. No shadows separated themselves from the doorways or alcoves where decorative tables sat. Time to be brave. She yanked her heels off and discarded them in the closet. Barefoot, she could run across the wood floor upstairs and the tile floor below without making a sound. She hurried out of the closet and rushed toward the back stairs. She figured those would be safer because only someone in the kitchen would see her on those stairs, and then only once she got to the bottom. The front stairs were too exposed and could be seen from most of the main rooms on the bottom floor.

She crept down the stairs, carefully listening for sounds of anyone who might be waiting for her. But everything was quiet. Too quiet. Where was Luke? And where was Grant?

When she reached the last step, she looked around the kitchen. Empty. She hurried to the doorway that led into the family room. Again, she paused, looking out at the massive room, but she didn't see anyone. Where had they gone?

Across the room she could see the foyer. With the front door standing wide open. Was it a trick? Was someone watching her even now, baiting her with the open door, the promise of escape?

*Where are you, Luke? Are you okay?*

She ducked back into the kitchen, debating her next steps. A weapon. She needed a weapon, something to defend herself with, or Luke, if it came to that. She ran to the butcher-block holder on the countertop and pulled out the biggest knife she could find. From tip to tip it had to be at least twelve inches long. The thought of wielding it against someone had her stomach twisting. She put the knife back and selected a smaller one, one that she could conceal the way Grant had. She would use it if she had to, but only as a last resort.

She slid the knife blade beneath the sleeve of her blouse and held the hilt in her palm. For the most part, the weapon was hidden, but she could pull it out quickly if needed. Then she pulled a small cast-iron skillet out from a cabinet. About five inches in diameter, it wasn't too heavy for her to hold, but it could do some serious damage if she had to swing it at someone's head.

That sickening image had her almost putting the skillet down, but she reminded herself there was someone else needing protection this time. It wasn't just about her. She had to be brave, and if that meant she had to hurt Grant, then that was what she'd have to do.

She crossed to the doorway again and looked into the family room. This time, she heard something. A taunting voice, low, familiar. And then a scream, quickly cut off. She blinked in confusion. The scream had sounded familiar, too. And it had sounded like a woman. Was someone else here?

She stepped into the family room. Movement to her left had her spinning around, holding up the skillet.

It was snatched from her grasp as Luke stepped in front of her, holding his finger to his lips to tell her to be quiet.

She flung her arms around his waist and gave him a tight hug before stepping back. The look of surprise on his face had her feeling foolish. But then he pulled her close and hugged her back. He leaned down and pressed his lips close to her ear.

"Glad you're okay, too, but you should have stayed upstairs in the closet. Or better yet," he whispered, "you should have gotten out of here and hid in the woods."

She shook her head and pulled back. "I'm not leaving you here alone. You'd better figure out a way to include me in your plans."

His brows lowered. "You promised."

"I know, but it wasn't a promise I should have given."

He obviously didn't like to hear that. He looked as though he was about to argue with her, when another noise reached them. It sounded like angry words, again, in a low, ominously familiar tone, followed by a loud thump, as if someone had been hit.

"Where's it coming from?" she whispered.

He pointed to the door at the end of the family room, one that led into a room next to the foyer.

He set the skillet down on a nearby end table. "I gave Grant the slip a few minutes ago and was going to come upstairs and get you. But then I saw him go into that room."

"The study," she whispered. "He's got someone else in there. A woman. He's hurting her. We can't leave her here."

His mouth thinned. "I know. Try to stay out of the way, okay? Can you at least promise you won't jump out in front of a gun or something?"

"I'm not an idiot."

He grinned. "No, you're not an idiot. You're beautiful, maddening and utterly adorable, but never an idiot."

She grinned back.

They hurried along the edge of the wall so the occupants of the study couldn't see them. When they reached the doorway, Luke motioned for her to stay there.

She nodded, content to trust that he knew what he was doing. If she saw an opening to help, she would. But he didn't need to know that. After all, she didn't want to distract him, as he'd said earlier.

Another scream sounded from inside the room, oddly muted, though.

She pressed her hand to her throat.

Luke's jaw tightened and he looked into the room. He stiffened, then hurriedly disappeared through the doorway.

Carol waited, but when he didn't immediately return, she crept forward and peeked inside. When she saw what Luke had seen, the knife she'd been holding concealed in her left hand fell from her numb fingers and clattered to the marble floor.

LUKE HAD JUST reached the chair where Grant was sitting, when he heard the sound behind him and knew Carol had come into the room. His heart broke for her, but at the same time he couldn't help her, not yet.

Grant didn't move in spite of the noise Carol had made. Instead, he held his head in his hands and wept. Luke rushed around the edge of the chair and grabbed the gun that Grant had placed on the end table. Grant lifted his head and gave him a bleary-eyed look.

"Go ahead," he rasped. "Shoot me. It doesn't matter now."

"Where's your knife?" Luke demanded, pointing the gun at him.

Another scream sounded from the tableau playing on the big-screen TV at the end of the room. Luke winced and forced himself not to look. He'd already seen more than he'd ever wanted to see when he entered the room.

"The knife," he prodded. "And for the love of God, turn the TV off."

Grant fumbled on his left side for the knife he'd apparently tucked into the cushion.

A whimper escaped from Carol.

Luke couldn't stand knowing what she was seeing. He couldn't wait for Grant to find the remote, either. He turned his gun and fired at the TV. The screen cracked and went dark, a burning smell rising through the room. Luke didn't care if the entire house burned down. At least Carol wasn't seeing the recording of herself anymore, being beaten and raped by her former husband.

Grant handed the knife to Luke. "I'm sorry, Caroline," he called out. "I didn't know. Why didn't you ever say anything?"

She crossed to the TV and took the video card out of the player beneath it before facing him. She clenched the card in her fist. "It was my shame, my burden, to share or not to share. And neither you nor Daniel ever made a secret of your dislike for me. I had no reason to think you would believe me, or help me, if I told you about Richard."

He wiped his eyes that were still streaming tears. "You were a waitress. We thought you married him for his money. But that doesn't mean we wouldn't have helped you if we'd…" He shook his head. "I didn't know. And after Richard was killed, I assumed you were behind it, that you'd paid someone to kill him. And once I heard about the will, I figured you must have switched the wills so you'd get all his money."

"Why did you break into the house back in town last

night?" Luke asked, risking a quick glance at Carol to see if she was okay. She was pale, but holding her own.

"I broke in because I knew Richard had those recorders all over the place. He was always paranoid like that. I was going to get the cards and watch them to see if any of them showed Caroline talking to someone about killing Richard, or talking about the will." He shook his head. "But it doesn't matter now. I don't care that you killed him. He deserved it for what he did to you. God, I'm so, so sorry." He covered his face with his hands again.

Carol's face had gone ashen as he spoke. "What other recorders?"

Luke held the gun on Grant and crossed the room to stand by her. "Answer the question."

Grant wiped his eyes and collapsed against the back of the chair. "Richard showed me one of the recorders once, a long time ago, at his office. He was trying to catch someone he thought was guilty of sharing corporate secrets with one of his competitors. He joked that he should use them at home, too, to make sure the staff wasn't helping themselves to the silver when he wasn't around. When I was visiting the mansion once, I searched the guest room I was in just to see if he was serious, and I found the camera hidden in the top dresser drawer— just like the camera hidden in his desk drawer at work. I always figured he had them in every room after that."

Luke reached out his left hand. Carol threaded her fingers with his and he gently squeezed.

"Carol isn't the one who had your brother killed," Luke said. He felt more than saw Carol's gaze on him. "I don't need to see the recordings to know that."

"Thank you," she murmured.

He nodded. "Grant, my phone's broken. Do you have a phone?"

Grant reached into his back pocket.

Luke stiffened. "Slowly."

Grant carefully pulled out the cell phone.

"Put it on the coffee table in the center of the room and then sit back down."

Grant did as he was told. When he was a safe distance away, Luke picked up the phone and handed it to Carol. "Will you call 911?"

She made the call, gave them the address, then sat on one of the couches with Luke, facing Grant.

"I think you made up that story about thinking Carol was behind your brother's death," Luke said. "*You're* the one who killed him. And you killed Mitch. Did you come here to kill Carol, too?"

Grant's eyes widened and he vigorously shook his head. "No, no, no. I swear. I would never hurt anyone. I didn't bring a gun with me here. I only took your gun away so you wouldn't shoot me."

"Right. And those were warning shots you fired at me."

"They were! I only came here to talk. I wanted the truth from Caroline."

"People who want to talk don't break into other people's houses and hit them over the head with a baseball bat."

His face flushed red. "I just wanted to overpower you so I could get your gun away and make you both sit down. I admit, I probably went about it the wrong way. But you have to understand. I thought she'd killed Richard, or had him killed, so I was afraid for my own life, too."

"I'm not buying any of this," Luke said.

"I am." Carol's soft voice called out beside him. "Grant has always been impulsive, and he's not much better than me at making the most well-thought-out, reasoned choices." She smiled sadly. "I also know you loved Richard deeply, even though you were both at odds with each other so much. You must have been overcome with grief thinking I had something to do with his death."

"You're being far kinder than I deserve," Grant said.

"I agree." Luke kept his gun trained on the other man.

"To be honest," Carol said, "I was half convinced you might have been the one who'd killed him."

"Me?" Grant's face reddened again. "Why would you think that? I loved Richard."

"I know, but you two argued so much."

He twisted his hands together. "We argued about money, a cardinal sin in his opinion. Money meant everything to him." His mouth tightened. "Even more than family."

Luke had had enough of Grant's whining and Carol's feeling sorry for him. The man had held a knife to Carol, twice. Even now there was a small smear of blood on her throat where his knife had pricked her. And his stunt on the balcony could have killed her if she'd let go before Luke could pull her back up. Grant didn't deserve her sympathy. He deserved a fist in the face, just for starters. "You said something about a will earlier. What were you talking about?"

The look Grant gave Carol wasn't anywhere near as sympathetic as it had been earlier. If anything, he looked bitter, angry, as if he'd hold that knife to her neck again if he got another chance.

Luke motioned with his gun, catching Grant's attention. "Don't look at her. Look at me, and answer my question."

"Why don't you ask her? She may have killed Richard, she may not have. I don't know. And I don't care anymore after watching that, that…" He waved at the broken

TV. "But it's not fair that she switched Richard's will. It doesn't matter how mad he was at me, he wouldn't have left me only five million dollars. And he didn't have any reason to be mad at Daniel and only leave him five million, too. I want to know where the real will is. The one that was filed with the court is fake."

Carol shook her head. "I don't know anything about a new will. All I know is that Richard drew one up shortly after we got married and I assume that's the one that was filed with the court."

"Why do you care about the will?" Luke asked. "You and your brother are both millionaires."

"Daniel's a millionaire, but not me. My money's all tied up in my company. In case you hadn't noticed, the economy has been rough for the past few years. I'm close to bankruptcy. And my daughter is ready to start college. Five million dollars is a Band-Aid. We're going to lose everything."

Sirens sounded outside the window, getting closer.

Grant's fingers tightened on the arm of his chair.

"Don't even think about it," Luke warned.

Grant cursed and sat back.

Carol had grown quiet. Once again she'd been put through more than anyone should have to bear. All Luke wanted to do was hold her and assure her that everything would be okay. But it would be a lie. Because he wasn't at all sure that it would be. Someone had murdered Richard Ashton. And someone had killed Mitch. Was that person Grant? Yes, probably. But if there was even a remote possibility that Grant was innocent, then the culprit was still out there, and Carol's life was still in danger.

The sirens stopped in front of the house, their lights flashing through the windows behind the ruined TV.

"I'll let them in." Carol crossed the room. She stopped

at the doorway and glanced down at the video card in her hand. She looked around, as if searching for something, and then held her hands up. It looked as if she was trying to bend the card in two, but she wasn't strong enough.

A rapid knock sounded on the front door. "Police. We had a 911 call from this address. Open up."

"Give me the card," Luke urged. "I'll destroy it for you." He wasn't sure if he was telling the truth or not. He didn't want to look at the video, and certainly didn't want anyone else to, but what if it contained evidence that would prove the identity of the killer?

Carol hurried to him but hesitated as she started to hand him the card. "Promise me you won't look at it and that you'll destroy it the first chance you get."

Guilt squeezed his throat, making it tight. He didn't want to give her his word when he wasn't sure yet what he was going to do. He didn't make promises lightly. And she didn't deserve to be lied to.

She frowned. "Luke?"

He cleared his throat, self-loathing nearly choking him. "Promise."

The look of relief that crossed her face had him silently cursing himself.

She handed him the card.

He shoved it into his pants pocket as she rushed out of the room to let the police inside.

## Chapter Ten

It took over an hour to sort out things at the house and for an EMT to stitch the wound on the side of Luke's head. He refused to go to the hospital, saying he was fine and that he wanted to keep guarding Carol until the police determined whether or not Grant was the killer.

When Luke and the police escort ushered Carol into the police station back in Savannah, the dull hum of noise quickly faded to an almost eerie silence. And when Carol saw one of the local gossip papers sitting on a table in the lobby area and saw her picture on the front page, she knew why. The caption underneath read DID WEALTHY, ABUSED SOCIALITE FINALLY GET HER REVENGE?

Luke's hand at her back tensed. He'd noticed the paper, too. Their eyes met and he shook his head, as if trying to tell her not to worry about it. She smiled, both to reassure him and to give the impression to anyone watching that she didn't care what others thought of her.

"In here." The police officer pushed a glass door open and waved them into an office. "Can I get you anything to eat or drink while you wait for Detective Cornell?"

Since the officer was looking at Carol, she shook her head. "I'm fine. Thank you."

"How long do you think Cornell will be?" Luke asked. He sat beside Carol in front of Cornell's desk.

"Depends on how the interview goes. As long as Ashton is talking, Cornell won't leave the room. You sure you want to wait?"

"Yes," they both said at the same time.

The officer left, closing the door behind him.

"Actually," Carol said, rising from her chair, "I wouldn't mind a moment in the ladies' room to freshen up."

Luke stood, too, and stepped to the door.

She put a hand on his arm. "I can handle this without you. We passed the ladies' room two doors down. And the place is crawling with police officers. I'll be perfectly safe."

He didn't want to let her leave without him, but she insisted.

"All right. But if you're gone more than a few minutes, I'm sending a policewoman in there after you."

"I'll keep that in mind." She smiled again and headed out.

Luke stood in the hallway outside Cornell's office watching her. She gave him a small wave and went into the ladies' room.

Once inside, she quickly saw to her needs. Then she pulled her cell phone out of her purse to take care of the real reason she'd wanted a moment of privacy. Since meeting Luke she'd been as honest as possible with him, except for keeping the details of her relationship with her husband as private as she could. But this one time she knew she couldn't make this call in front of him because he would have argued and tried to stop her.

The phone rang twice, then a man's deep voice answered. "Hello?"

"Hello, it's me, Carol Ashton."

"Is everything okay? Luke called me earlier and told me what happened at the house in the country."

"Yes, yes, we're both fine. Actually, we're at the police station. Cornell took Grant Ashton to an interview room and he's talking to him right now."

"Good. I hope Ashton tells Cornell everything."

"I don't."

"Excuse me?"

"That's why I called. I don't want Grant telling Cornell *anything*. I need your help."

HALF AN HOUR LATER, Cornell stepped into his office and greeted Carol and Luke before sitting behind his desk. "Looks like we've got our man."

"He confessed?" Luke asked.

"Sort of. He admits he's the one who broke into the Ashton mansion here in town the other night and left Mrs. Ashton dangling off the balcony."

Carol shuddered at the memory and gripped her hands together in her lap.

"He also said he moved the GPS tracking device from Mrs. Ashton's car to your Thunderbird because he figured if Mrs. Ashton went anywhere she'd be with you."

"How did he know where the tracker was in the first place?" Luke asked.

"I get the impression he and his brother Richard used to quite close. He knew a lot of his secrets." Cornell glanced at Carol and his face turned a light shade of red. "Apparently not all of them, though. He insisted quite emphatically that he didn't know what your husband… did to you, or he would have tried to help you."

"I believe him," she said. "I didn't realize back then that he would have helped, or I might have told him. But after seeing how upset he was earlier, I do believe he would have tried to stop my husband."

Cornell folded his arms on his desk. "He mentioned a

video, and that Luke shot the TV at the country house to stop the video. But no one found a DVD or video card. Do either of you know what happened to it?"

"What else did he tell you?" Luke asked, avoiding the question.

Carol shot him a grateful look.

Cornell studied both of them, obviously debating whether to press the issue of the missing video. Finally, he said, "Grant gave us details about how he tracked you to the house in the country. He insists he only did so because he was convinced Mrs. Ashton had arranged for Richard to be killed and he wanted a chance to confront her about it. He swore he never meant to hurt either of you."

Luke pointed to the side of his head where he had a brand-new row of stitches. "I'd like to offer evidence to the contrary."

"Noted, I assure you. The gist of what he said was that he wanted to confront Carol both about the murder and about his brother's will. He's convinced there's another will somewhere and that Mrs. Ashton knows where it is."

"Did Grant say anything about killing Mitch?" Luke asked.

"He insists he had nothing to do with that, or his brother's death. His financial difficulties are a strong motive for him killing his brother. He assumed Richard would bequeath him a substantial part of his fortune, and he was bitterly surprised when that didn't happen. As for Mitch, we haven't come up with a motive yet but the evidence supports the possibility that Grant killed him."

Carol straightened in her chair. "What evidence?"

"One of the people at the cemetery remembered seeing Grant and Mitch arguing before the service started.

Grant was apparently upset about Mitch taking pictures. I don't know whether there was more to it than that, or whether that would be enough to make Grant turn violent. But from what we're gleaning from other interviews with Grant's friends and known associates, he has a temper and tends to act without thinking first. Plus, he's known to carry a pocketknife. The coroner said a small knife, like a pocketknife, was used to kill Mr. Brody."

Luke winced.

Carol offered him a sympathetic smile before turning back to Cornell. "I thought you said Grant might be Richard's killer. It doesn't sound to me like you have any evidence of that."

Cornell smiled and put his hands behind his head. "That's because I saved the best part for last. You told me at the country house that Grant and Richard argued quite a bit. I was able to subpoena Grant's credit-card records and already got a hit that puts a whole new light on things."

He sat forward, resting his arms on his desk. "The morning of Richard Ashton's murder, Grant Ashton filled up at a gas station…two miles from the cottage where Ashton was murdered. Lucky for us, that station is brand-new, with state-of-the-art electronic video surveillance. They keep their recordings on a hard drive, which means they can store them for months without running out of space and writing over them again like some of the cheaper equipment does. I've got someone on the way there right now to review the recordings from the morning of the murder. I think we all know who we're going to see on that video."

He pushed himself up from his chair and straightened his jacket. "Now, if you'll excuse me. I think I've let my subject stew long enough. I'm about to go get that confession."

A knock sounded on the door.

"Come in," Cornell called out.

A police officer opened the door and stood back. Alex Buchanan walked in wearing a suit and holding a briefcase.

Luke and Carol stood.

"I didn't know you were coming to the station," Luke said. "Did your investigator find something out about the case?"

"Unfortunately, no."

"Then why are you here?"

He glanced at Carol before crossing to Cornell. "I've been notified that you have a client of mine in custody and that you're interviewing him without his lawyer present. I'm here to stop the interview and confer with my client."

A look of confusion crossed Cornell's face. "But the only person I'm interviewing right now is Grant Ashton."

"He's my client."

"He hasn't asked for a lawyer," Cornell insisted.

"A family member hired me to represent him."

Cornell crossed his arms across his chest. "Oh? Who? His brother, Daniel?"

"That information is confidential."

Cornell argued with Alex about having the right to know who was trying to make things so difficult for him.

Luke wasn't paying attention to either of them. Instead, he was intently watching *her.*

She cleared her throat. "Gentlemen." When Cornell continued to shout, she cleared her throat louder. "Detective, Alex, please. I think I can clear up this…misunderstanding."

Cornell gave her an aggravated look. "Oh? And how can you do that?"

"I'm the family member who hired Alex."

CORNELL'S PREVIOUSLY COOPERATIVE attitude ended the moment Carol told him she'd asked Alex to represent her brother-in-law. He ushered her and Luke out of his office and ordered them to wait down the hall in a conference room while he and Alex went to see Grant.

Once inside, Luke shut the door and pulled a chair out for Carol. He crossed to the other side of the table, but rather than sit, he flattened his palms on the table and leaned down toward her.

"What was that all about?" he growled.

She calmly picked up her purse and stood. She was all the way to the door before he realized she was actually leaving. He rushed around the table and caught up to her in the hallway.

"What are you doing?" he demanded.

"Leaving."

He rolled his eyes. "Yeah, got that. *Why* are you leaving?"

Her knuckles whitened from where she gripped her purse so tightly. "I spent nearly five years cowering from a man who used his size and strength to intimidate and hurt me. Those days are over."

She tried to move past him.

He reached out toward her.

She flinched and backed up.

Luke froze, his hand in midair. The anger drained out of him as understanding dawned. "Carol, I was just going to fix your purse strap. It's about to fall off your shoulder."

Her face flushed and she grabbed the strap just as the purse started to fall.

Luke took a step back to give her some more space. "I thought you knew I would never hurt you."

Her blue eyes rose to his and he was shocked at the anger that flashed in them. "Yes, I do know that. Because I won't let you, or any man, hurt me. Ever. Again."

He scrubbed his jaw with his hands. "I'm sorry. I don't know what else to say. Was I using my size back there to intimidate you? Yeah, I guess I was. My size is an asset in my line of work. I use it to my advantage automatically, without even thinking about it. But I never should have done that with you. It won't happen again."

She glanced uncertainly past him.

He held his hand out toward the door. "We need to talk. Please."

The seconds ticked by like minutes and Luke was worried he'd screwed up beyond her ability to forgive. How could he have been so stupid, knowing her past? If he could kick his own ass he would.

She took a step toward the conference room but stopped at the sound of footsteps.

Alex Buchanan turned the corner and headed toward them. "Are you two leaving?"

Luke raised a brow and waited for Carol to make that decision.

"No, we were just going back into the conference room," she said.

"Mind if I join you?"

"Of course not."

Luke would have rather had a private conversation with her, but since he didn't have a choice, he followed the two of them back into the room and closed the door.

Alex leaned his forearms on the table. "Grant gave me permission to share what he and I discussed, but you hired me, Carol. Do you want me to share the information in private or can Luke be included?"

"Of course he can be included. Please, tell us what you found out."

Carol's quick agreement to include Luke had some of his earlier worry fading.

"Okay," Alex said. "But first, I'm curious to know why you hired me in the first place. You never really explained that on the phone."

"The phone? When did you have a chance to call him?" Luke asked.

Her face turned a light pink. "I wasn't with you every single minute since we got to the station."

Luke frowned, then enlightenment dawned. She'd called Alex from the bathroom. He grinned but decided to stay quiet so he wouldn't embarrass her further.

"I hired you because it was the right thing to do. Grant isn't the killer—"

"You don't know that," Luke insisted.

"Yes. I do. I've known Grant for a long time. And while I may not know a great deal about his personal life and what makes him tick, I do know one thing for certain. When he gets upset, he lets everything out. There's no holding back. He doesn't know how to be clever or coy. Back at the country house, his emotions were raw. He was telling the truth when he said he didn't kill Richard. It isn't right for him to be railroaded into prison. And it especially isn't right that his wife and daughter should suffer, either."

Luke watched her intently. "I notice you haven't said anything about your other brother-in-law during all this time. Do you feel Daniel's innocent, too?"

She frowned. "Honestly, I have no idea. Daniel is more…self-contained than Grant. He's always treated me politely, respectfully. But he didn't come to the mansion very often. I really don't know that much about him except that he's not married. Daniel and Grant are in many ways opposites. With Grant, you know what you're getting. With Daniel, he's all manners and self-control." She rubbed her hands up and down her arms. "Richard was very controlled, too. I guess that's one of the reasons I can't come to any conclusions about Daniel. They seemed so much alike."

"Well, Cornell is looking into both of them," Alex said. "He was excited, hoping he'd caught his man earlier, but he's keeping an open mind and making sure his team explores every possible lead."

"What all did Grant tell you?" Luke asked.

"He reiterated what he'd already told Cornell. He basically admitted to breaking into both houses and assaulting both of you."

"I don't want to press charges for that," Carol said.

Luke cursed.

Alex shot him a warning look. "That's for you to discuss with Cornell. It would be a conflict of interest for me to talk about that. I will, however, tell you that Grant's main hang-up seems to be about the will. He's convinced the will that was filed was fake and that his brother wouldn't have left him only five million dollars. He wanted me to try to get a search warrant for the mansion. He's convinced the will is hidden inside."

"Would a judge go along with that?" Luke asked.

"Highly unlikely, and that's what I told Grant. Unless he has some kind of proof, no judge will want to get embroiled in that kind of mess. When I told him that, he got upset and said he should hire Leslie Harrison to represent him. He said Leslie represented Richard in a dispute with the IRS last year and won. He figured if she could beat the IRS, she could get a judge to look into the will. I reminded him Harrison isn't a criminal lawyer. I also told him if she was his lawyer I wouldn't be. I've never cared much for Miss Harrison and how she does business and I don't want to be associated with her professionally."

Carol frowned. "What's he going to do?"

"I don't know. He's in an odd state of mind right now, hard to reason with. I think he knows more than he's telling. I know you want me to protect him, but he's his own worst enemy. Hopefully my warnings to him to not say anything else to Cornell will sink in. I'll come back in the morning and talk to him after he's had a chance to sleep on everything."

Alex stood to leave. "Oh, I almost forgot. Cornell said to tell you that you're free to go. His lead detective wanted to discuss the investigation with him and he wasn't sure how late he'd be. He'll call you if he has more questions about what happened today."

"Thank you, Alex," Carol said. "For everything."

"My pleasure." He shook their hands and left.

Luke sat back in his chair and considered Carol. "We've had an incredibly full night and day. Any idea where you want to go this time? As your bodyguard, I'm advising you not to go to any of your husband's holdings, no matter how much you believe no one knows about them. And I think we need to pick up a rental car just to be sure no other GPS trackers are hanging around."

"I'll leave the destination up to you this time. I'd like nothing better than one night without worrying about some madman finding me. But first, we need to stop at the mansion here in town."

"To get more clothes?"

"No. To get Richard's will."

## Chapter Eleven

It was late afternoon by the time Luke and Carol arrived at the mansion, or at least, arrived a block away and parked on a side street while they surveyed the mass of news vans and reporters surrounding the estate.

"Good grief," Carol said. "The press has never been this bad before."

"Murder sells." He glanced at his watch. "We're five minutes early. Are you sure you want to go in there? We can leave right now, rent a car, hole up in a hotel somewhere."

"A hotel hardly seems like the place to hide out. I'd think the paparazzi have lookouts all over town. A hotel is one of the first places they'd expect me to go."

"Not if you're in disguise."

"Hmm. Maybe. But the point is moot for now. Because I'm not going anywhere but the mansion. I have to find that will."

"You've been secretive about the alleged will since dropping that bomb on me back at the police station. I think now is a good time to explain why you're suddenly so sure there *is* another will."

"It just makes sense. The more I think about it, the more I'm convinced that Richard would never leave his fortune to me, not after the first six months of our marriage, at least. I wasn't…important to him as a person. I was an object, his property, to control. He wouldn't have wanted to risk leaving his legacy to me. He wouldn't expect I'd be intelligent enough or capable enough to keep his businesses on the right track. He would have left the bulk of the estate to his brothers. Which means, there must be another will inside, in his papers somewhere."

"Possible, but he had Leslie as his personal lawyer on retainer. Why not file the will if he went to the trouble of drawing up another one?"

"Good question."

"I'm not sure I understand why you'd want to find the will, assuming it exists."

"What do you mean?"

"You're a billionaire. If what you say about an alternate will is true, you could lose everything. Why would you risk that?"

"Because it wouldn't be right. If the money belongs to someone else, they should have it."

"We're talking about Grant and Daniel here. Grant tried to kill you—"

"Allegedly."

"He held a freaking knife to your throat. Twice. He left you dangling off a balcony."

She winced. "Okay. Good points."

"And Daniel hasn't exactly come around to check on his beloved widowed sister-in-law after news of Richard's treatment of you leaked to the press. Neither of them seem particularly deserving of a massive change in fortune. On the other hand, you lived through hell and deserve every penny."

She looked out the windshield. "I can see where you might feel that way. But it's not like I could ever enjoy the money, knowing what I went through to get it. Don't you see? Everything I have reminds me of Richard." She held up her carefully manicured nails. "He dictated the color of my nail polish and how long my nails should be." She grabbed a handful of her long hair and held it up. "I'm a natural brunette. I never wanted to be blonde, but Richard wanted my hair this color. These clothes—" she waved her hand toward the silky pantsuit she wore "—these clothes were all chosen by Richard. All I want is to resolve this case so I can be safe once and for all. And then I want to go away somewhere, anywhere, someplace that doesn't remind me of him. If I buy another house, or new clothes, I'm buying them with his money. How will I ever truly escape him that way?"

Luke gently pushed her hair out of her eyes. "I always seem to say or do the wrong thing around you. It's none of my business what you do with the money or how you choose to live your life. You don't owe me any explanations."

She took his hand in hers. "You've been nothing but kind to me. You don't deserve to be lambasted for asking an obvious question." She shook her head. "But I just want to make sure the rightful owner of the money gets it. I want to be done with it so nothing ever comes back to haunt me later. I want to be free."

"You will be. Soon."

"I hope so. Too much has happened too fast. I just want to search the obvious places in the mansion to see if I can find a will. And then I want to get out of here. We can go wherever you think we'll be safe and won't be bothered by the press."

"Okay. Leave that to me. This won't be the first time I've had to sneak a client out from under watchful eyes and take them to a safe house." He glanced in the rearview mirror. "Here they come. Get ready. As soon as the press realizes what's happening, they'll be all over us."

She clutched her purse in her hand and grasped the door handle. "I'm ready."

A black Suburban pulled up beside them per the plan. Another one pulled up behind them. The doors popped open and half a dozen Stellar Security guards jumped out, surrounding Carol as she got out of the car.

Just as Luke had predicted, the press saw the Suburbans and started running toward them, aiming their cameras in their direction.

Carol hopped into the lead truck and it took off toward the mansion. Luke cursed and tossed the two bags that contained his and Carol's clothes into the back of the second truck and jumped in.

"Hurry up," he growled as the woman he was supposed to be guarding pulled farther away.

CAROL SLID THE bottom drawer of Richard's desk closed and plopped down in his leather chair. She'd searched every place she could think of for another will but hadn't found anything. At this point, she was inclined to think maybe Luke was right. Grant was just desperate for funds and had convinced himself the will that had been filed was a fake.

Luke walked into the office and propped himself on the edge of the desk. "I searched the master bedroom like you asked, top to bottom. Nothing. Even the wall safe is empty."

"Empty? It wasn't locked?"

"No. I pulled on the door handle and it opened right up. I assumed you'd given Cornell and his men the combination when they searched the room the other day and they didn't relock it." He frowned. "You didn't?"

She shook her head. "No. I don't even know the combination. But Richard put papers in that safe all the time. I find it hard to believe he would have left it unlocked. And I've never known it to be empty."

Luke pulled out his cell phone. "I'll update Cornell. See if he dusted the safe for prints. If he did, and didn't get any besides Richard's, I'll ask him to send a crew out here again and dust every inch of the thing. And then we're getting out of here. Is there anything you need if we don't come back for several days?"

"No. My bag from when we went to the country house has everything I need."

"All right. Wait here. I'll make that call, and then I'll arrange our escape from the press."

Luke hurried out of the room and waved down one of the housemaids. He made his request and a moment later she came back with an envelope and a sheet of paper. He thanked her, explained what he wanted to do to get Carol safely out of the house, and she ran off again to do what he'd asked.

He was going to call Cornell, but first he had two other calls to make. And since he didn't want anyone to overhear him, he hurried to the little glassed-in garden off the back of the house that Carol had shown him a few days ago during the house tour. There was a fountain in the middle of the garden that splashed and made enough noise that he felt confident no hidden cameras or spying servants would hear his conversations.

First, he called Trudy at the office. She commiserated with him over Mitch's death, which made him feel guilty because he hadn't thought much about Mitch with everything else that was going on. He didn't have time to grieve for his friend right now, so he forced the emotions aside and gently brought Trudy back to the task at hand. He explained what he needed in detail and had her repeat it back to him. Satisfied she would give his message to his men so they could set his escape plan in motion, he hung up and made his second call.

To Alex.

Guilt gnawed at him again as he waited for Alex to answer. What he was about to do would horrify Carol if she ever found out. He'd made a promise to her, and he'd assured her he never broke his promises. And up to this point, he never had. But after what she'd told him about the safe, he knew they were on borrowed time.

Whoever was behind Richard's death had also managed to break into the house and empty Richard's safe without anyone knowing, which meant the killer was most likely someone Carol knew and quite possibly trusted. It was Luke's duty to keep her safe, which meant—in this one instance—he needed to break his promise, because it very well might mean that he would find out the killer's identity.

"Alex Buchanan," the voice answered on the phone.

"It's Luke. I have to make this fast. First, can you ask your investigator to look into Stellar Security?"

"Okay. What's he supposed to look for?"

"Anything suspicious, anything to do with the Ashtons. I'm getting a weird feeling about Stellar. There have been too many security breaches with them supposedly in charge."

"All right. You said 'first.' What else did you need?"

"A huge favor. I'm going to leave something for you in a van later today. The keys will be under the front bumper in a hide-a-key box. I'm leaving you an envelope under the driver's seat." He gave Alex the address of where the van would be.

"Okay. And what am I supposed to do with this envelope?"

"I'm hopeful you can examine the evidence inside it and let me know if you can figure out who broke into the safe in the Ashtons' master bedroom. I have a feeling whoever broke into the safe is Richard Ashton's killer."

"And just what is this evidence that you want me to look at instead of the police?"

Luke glanced around to make sure no one had come into the garden. Then he reached into his pocket and pulled out the video card Carol had given him back at the country house.

## Chapter Twelve

An hour later, Cornell's CSI team was upstairs dusting the master-bedroom safe and the wall surrounding it, just in case they'd missed any prints the first time. Moments later, a housemaid and one of the Stellar Security guards—dressed in Carol's and Luke's clothes—ran out front to the circular driveway and hopped into the Rolls-Royce, sandwiched between two black Suburbans.

The caravan took off and barreled onto the street.

Just as Luke expected, the press made a mad dash to follow, and soon most of the news vans were racing after the decoy.

Some of the reporters remained, perhaps to ensure their counterparts hadn't been fooled. But they expected the wealthy socialite would leave the mansion in luxury, driven in one of the estate's expensive cars. They didn't pay attention to the pretty young housemaid and coarsely dressed gardener who left by way of the servants' entrance a few minutes later, walking hand in hand down the sidewalk.

When Luke and Carol in their disguises rounded the corner of the next street a couple of blocks over, another Stellar Security truck was waiting for them. They jumped in and rode in the truck a couple of miles away. Then the driver pulled over next to a dark blue Dodge Charger.

"Are you sure you want to do this, ma'am?" the driver asked. "Our company is more than capable of providing the security you need." His disdainful look wasn't lost on Luke.

Luke shrugged. "Up to you, Carol. They've done a smashup job so far." He didn't bother to temper the sarcasm in his voice.

She shook her head. "No, thank you. We're sticking to our original plan."

She got out, and Luke followed with their bags. Another security guard got out of the Charger and tossed the keys to Luke. He and Carol got inside, but as soon as the security van turned the corner, they hopped back out. They ran across the street to the parking garage on the corner and ducked inside.

"Where is it?" Carol asked.

"Two rows over, the white van on the end."

They hurried to the van and Luke grabbed the hide-a-key from under the front bumper. He slid open the side door behind the driver's seat, tossed in their bags and helped Carol inside. The windows were tinted dark just as Luke had insisted when he'd called two of his men to help him arrange the second half of the escape plan, unbeknownst to Stellar Security. He and Carol changed their clothes, using the clothing his men had gotten for them—T-shirts and jeans.

Carol finished putting her hair into a ponytail, then grinned as she ran her hands over the soft jeans covering her legs. "Richard would have been appalled to see me wearing something so…common."

Luke smiled, her restored good mood infectious. "That doesn't seem to bother you."

"Nope. Not one bit."

Not content with just one car change, Luke drove them

a few more miles outside the historic district of Savannah and they traded cars again. This time they drove a black Camaro.

A few minutes later, with Carol in disguise so no one would recognize her, they signed in at the Hyatt Regency just off River Street as Mr. and Mrs. Carl Johnson.

CAROL WAS LAUGHING when they ran into their hotel suite. "That was so much fun. No one knew who I was! We walked past that reporter in the lobby and he looked right through me."

Luke smiled and set their bags beside the couch. "You should smile more often."

"Yes. I should!" But her smile faded when he took a straight-backed chair from the table in the kitchenette and propped it under the doorknob.

But he didn't stop there.

He grabbed two drinking glasses, wrapped them in a dish towel, then set them on the floor. He stomped on them, startling Carol as the glass shattered beneath his shoe.

"Sorry," he said. "I should have warned you."

"No problem," she murmured as she watched him take the towel that was now full of broken glass to the door.

He dumped the contents on the floor and used his shoe to spread it around. He double-checked the locks and made sure the security bar was in place on the door. Then he made a full circuit of the room, even checking into the cabinets in the tiny kitchen.

Carol shook her head in bewilderment as he stood on a chair and checked the air-conditioning vents.

"You don't honestly think someone could wiggle themselves into the room through those tiny vents, do you?"

"No. But they could get a camera in there."

The last of her happy mood died a quick death.

He passed her and headed into the bedroom.

She followed, curious to see what else he thought was necessary to ensure her safety and privacy. One thing was certain: none of the Stellar Security guards had ever gone to this kind of trouble for her. Luke's thoroughness made the danger she was in feel more real than ever, but it also made her feel surprisingly safe and protected. No ill-timed picture was going to leak to the press under Luke's watch, giving away their location to the killer.

After checking beneath the bed and inside the closets, as well as the vents, Luke headed into the bathroom. Carol stood in the open doorway and watched him rap on the mirror over the sink, and then cup his hands against the mirror and press his face up against his hands.

"Why are you doing that?" she asked.

He straightened. "The mirror is on the wall that's shared with the next room, so I'm making sure it's not two-way glass."

"You've got to be kidding. No one even knows I'm here. It's not like the paparazzi are in the next room trying to catch a picture of me taking a shower."

"You'd be amazed at some of the lengths they go to for a picture that can earn them thousands of dollars. If a paparazzo bribed the desk clerk downstairs to send us to this room if we came into the hotel, and the clerk recognized us, we could be on camera right now."

She glanced at the mirror and shivered. "But we're not. Right?"

He shook his head. "No, we're not. This suite is as secure as I can make it." He patted the gun in the holster concealed beneath his leather jacket. "And if the worst happens, I can still protect you. Don't worry."

"I'm not worried, surprisingly. I think I may even be

able to sleep tonight without nightmares. I'm exhausted."
She glanced around, noting there was only one bed.

Luke's mouth crooked up in a half smile. "I didn't want
to blow our married-couple cover or I'd have asked for
two beds. I can sleep on the couch."

"Don't be silly. You're far too tall for the couch. And,
honestly, I'm way too tired to want to sleep on an un-
comfortable couch myself. The bed is plenty big enough
for both of us."

His brows rose. "Are you sure?"

"Of course. We're both adults. I'm sure we can be-
have ourselves. Now, if you'll excuse me, I'm going to
take a shower."

SLEEPING TOGETHER WAS a terrible idea.

Luke lay awake long after Carol's breathing had turned
deep and even. He was tired and badly needed to get some
sleep so he would be alert tomorrow. Or at least, he *was*
tired until he'd turned on his side facing her and had noticed how the sliver of moonlight coming in through the
curtain traced the soft, delicate curve of her cheek. Or
how she made a sexy little moaning sound in her sleep
when she shifted her legs, making her long, white nightgown ride up high on her silky thighs, on skin that was
flawless.

*Except for the bruises.*

Even in the dark he could see the outlines of the fading
marks her husband had left on her upper arms, her thighs.
His hands clenched into fists and he rolled onto his back
to stare up at the ceiling. The minutes dragged by.

"Luke?"

He turned his head on the pillow. Carol was facing him
and staring at him. He had to force himself not to look

down where her neckline gaped, revealing far more of her generous curves than she probably realized.

"Sorry," he whispered. His voice came out a harsh croak. He cleared his throat. "Didn't mean to wake you."

Her delicate brows arched. "It's okay. Is something wrong?"

*Yes.* "No, of course not. Go back to sleep. I'll try to stop moving around so much."

He closed his eyes and tried to think of anything but the beautiful woman lying beside him, or how she smelled like flowers, or that some of her hair was lying across his right shoulder. His fingers curled into his palms against the urge to thread his fingers through the glorious, curly mass.

The bed shifted and he could have sworn she'd moved closer. He could feel her heat curling around him, making him want to pull her closer.

"Luke."

His eyes flew open. He cautiously turned his head and almost groaned out loud. She *was* closer, almost touching. Her face was just inches from his. All he had to do was roll over and their lips would meet.

He stared at the ceiling again. "Yes?" he rasped.

Her hand slid tentatively across his chest.

He sucked in a sharp breath and looked at her. "Carol, what are you doing?"

She snatched her hand back. "I'm sorry. I thought maybe... I shouldn't have done that."

He grabbed her hand, immediately softening his hold when her eyes widened with alarm. He slowly, ever so gently, pulled her hand toward him and placed it back on his chest. If she was any other woman, he'd know exactly what to do right now. He'd interpret that hand as meaning she wanted him, and he knew exactly what to do about *that*. But this was Carol. She was far too good for some-one like him, and innocent in every way that mattered.

Her husband had hurt her so much. She probably didn't even realize how her touch frustrated him and made him want her. And even if that wasn't a consideration, he was her bodyguard. He needed to stay focused. Sleeping with a client was a huge no-no on so many levels.

So instead of pulling her to him and covering her lips with his, instead of sliding his hand down her back, across her hips, and cupping her round bottom against his growing erection, he kept an iron-tight control on his desires.

"You said you thought…something. What did you think, exactly?" he asked, unable to speak above a rough whisper in spite of his good intentions.

Her hand fluttered beneath his. He reluctantly let it go and she pulled it back. She propped her head on her palm, her gaze falling to his lips.

"I met…*him*…when I was innocent," she whispered. "I've never…been with anyone…else. But with him, it wasn't… I mean, in the beginning it was very, but then…" She closed her eyes, her voice sighing out on a shaky breath before she opened her eyes again. "I don't want to be hurt again."

He waited for her to say more, but she seemed to be struggling for words, and if her face got any redder it might burst into flames. He rolled onto his side and cupped his face in his palm, mirroring her posture. He put his other hand on the bed between them, palm up.

She slowly slid her hand across the sheet and looped her fingers with his.

"Carol?"

"Yes?"

"I would never hurt you."

A single tear slid down her cheek. "I know," she whispered.

"If I was going to make love to you," he whispered, "I'd take it slow. I'd be gentle and incredibly…thorough. I'd make sure you enjoyed every touch, every stroke, every kiss. But I'm not going to make love to you tonight."

Her eyes had widened during his little speech, and now she ran her tongue over her lips.

His groin tightened painfully.

"Why not?" she whispered.

The disappointment in her voice had him reaching for her before he realized what he was doing. He stopped himself and dropped his hand.

"Because it's unethical, wrong. You're my client. I'm your bodyguard. A relationship between us is impossible while I'm guarding you."

A smile hovered on her tempting mouth. "Okay. Then consider yourself fired. I'll rehire you in the morning."

He laughed, delighted that she still had a sense of humor after everything she'd been through. Then he sobered. "I'm serious. It would be wrong. I'd be taking advantage of you. Being in danger together forces a kind of false intimacy. It can be an aphrodisiac, but it's not real."

Her smile turned bitter. "I was in danger the whole time I was married. Trust me, it wasn't an aphrodisiac." She reached for his hand. "I want you, Luke. And I haven't wanted anyone in a very long time. If you don't want me, tell me. But if you do, then don't throw logic and reason between us."

He disengaged his hand from hers and lightly traced his finger down the curve of her cheek. "I want you, too, very much. But I don't want you to hate me later."

She shook her head. "I won't." She dropped her gaze

and bit her bottom lip. "But I'm still scared, even though I want you."

He fought a war with his conscience, but the battle didn't last long. He wanted her too much to keep denying the attraction between them. But he didn't want her frightened. He couldn't bear that.

"There's no reason to be scared," he whispered. "You're the one who's in control."

"I am?"

"Yes." He lowered his hand back to the bed. "I won't move unless you want me to. You can touch me, or not. Kiss me, or don't. It's your decision." He rolled onto his back and put his hands behind his head, striking a relaxed pose he was far from feeling. He wanted nothing more than to cover her body with his, to explore every fascinating dip and curve. But he knew that wasn't what she needed, and he sensed she wouldn't respond to that. Not yet, not with her fledgling desire warring with her instinctive fear because of her past.

She flexed her fingers on the sheet, as if debating whether to touch him. "Will you take off your shirt?" she asked.

In answer, he pulled his shirt off and dropped it to the floor, then put his hands behind his head again.

She glanced uncertainly at him, then slowly, so slowly it made him ache, she feathered her fingers up his side, leaving a burning trail in their wake. Growing bolder, she ran her hands across his ribs, testing the muscles there, exploring like an innocent who'd never been allowed the freedom he was giving her.

And maybe she hadn't. Not for the first time, Luke wished he could have met Richard Ashton in another century, when a man could defend a woman's honor on a dueling field. He would have loved to challenge the monster to a duel for the brutal way he'd used and abused this kind, beautiful, caring woman.

Her hand stilled on his abdomen and she looked at him uncertainly. He realized his thoughts of vengeance against her former husband had made him tense. He forced himself to relax and give her an encouraging smile.

Her tentative smile answered his, and soon she was killing him again with the warm slide of her hand across his heated skin. She seemed particularly fascinated with the vee formed by his abdominal muscles and how the dark line of hair disappeared beneath the sheet.

He'd worn his jeans to bed, to preserve her modesty. If he hadn't, there'd be no question on her part about how much he wanted her right now.

She slid up in the bed until her lips were close to his again. "Luke, may I...kiss you?"

"Carol, you can do whatever you want."

She let out a puff of laughter. "Okay, then I'd really like you to take off your jeans, and maybe take a *little* bit of control—because I feel silly now and I don't know what to do next."

He brought his hands down from behind his head and gently cupped her face. Then he slowly, carefully, pulled her down to him, with her on top, in control, and pressed her lips to his.

He kept the kiss gentle, soft, or at least he tried to. But he'd wanted her for so long that the feel of her softness against his had him shaking with need. He deepened the kiss, and when her lips parted, he swept his tongue inside, teasing, tasting, teaching her to kiss him back.

She moaned deep in her throat and dug her nails into his shoulder as she half covered him with her body, her breasts pressed against his chest, burning him through her thin nightgown. Suddenly she pulled back and stared at him, her blue eyes nearly black in the dark room, but wide as if she was stunned.

He reached up and traced his thumb over her full bottom lip. "Are you okay? Do you want to stop?"

She shook her head, her hair bouncing across her shoulders. "I don't want to stop." She reached down between them and tugged at his waistband. "But we aren't going to be able to do much more with you still wearing these."

He arched a brow. "I'll take mine off if you take yours off."

She arched a brow in response. "I'll see your bet and raise you, sir." She rolled off him and stood on her side of the bed. Suddenly her white nightgown fluttered down on top of him, covering his face.

He pulled it off his face just in time to see her fully nude body diving beneath the sheet. She lay back on her pillow beside him with the sheet pulled all the way up to her neck.

Her shyness was his reminder that he was going to have to take it slow.

This was going to be an agonizingly long night. But he was going to enjoy every minute of it. And he was going to make sure *she* enjoyed every minute of it.

He slid out from under the covers and was about to shuck off his jeans and underwear when he realized he didn't have any condoms. He stood in indecision.

"Is something wrong?" she asked, sounding worried that maybe he'd changed his mind about wanting her.

He briefly closed his eyes, his body in agony at the thought of what he was going to have to *not* do. "We can't do this," he said, even as he pulled out his wallet, hoping against hope that there was a condom in there. But since he wasn't in the habit of one-night stands and his last long-term relationship had ended over a year ago, he didn't hold out much hope.

"Oh. I see. Well, I'm sorry. I shouldn't have assumed you wanted— That is, I…" She let out a deep breath. "Just forget it."

His head jerked up.

She rolled over and faced the other wall.

He cursed himself for being an idiot. He rushed to the other side of the bed and squatted down at eye level. "It's not that I don't want you. Never, ever think that." And just to be sure she believed him, he kissed her. And this time, he didn't hold back. He pressed her against the pillow, half reclining on the bed, his mouth covering hers as he poured all his desire for her into that one hot, wet kiss. He stroked her tongue with his and she moaned deep in her throat again, shoving her hands into his hair and pulling him harder against her.

When they broke apart, they were both gasping for air. He felt her heart slamming in her chest against his, which was racing just as hard.

"I don't…understand," she said between deep, rasping breaths. "Why can't we, you know…?"

"Because I don't have any protection," he whispered, bending down and lightly sucking the side of her neck.

She arched off the bed and panted his name. "Protection? You showed me your gun earlier."

He laughed against the side of her neck. "Not that kind of protection, love. I don't have a condom."

Her eyes widened and then she laughed. He thought it was the most beautiful sound in the world.

She pulled him to her and this time *she* kissed *him*. It was even hotter and wilder than the last kiss. By the time they broke apart, his jeans were so tight he thought he would die.

"You're wicked to tease me so mercilessly when we can't go any further," he complained.

"Oh, we're definitely going further. You're going to get some condoms."

He shook his head. "No, can't risk leaving the suite. It's late now. The odds are much higher someone would notice us and might recognize you. Earlier, there were other people in the lobby and we were able to blend in."

"Us? *You* can go downstairs and get what we need. I assume they have them in the men's bathroom? I'll just wait here."

"No. I'm not leaving you. End of discussion."

She arched a brow and shoved him back. Then she slowly and deliberately pulled the sheet down to rest beneath her breasts. Her perfect, mouthwatering, beautiful breasts with little pink buds just begging for his kisses.

"You're not being fair," he groaned, unable to even pretend to lift his gaze from her bountiful display.

She chucked him under the chin, forcing him to meet her gaze. "Condoms. Find a way."

He wrenched his gaze from her body and looked around the room. He practically dived at the phone beside the bed. He pressed every button he could find in the dark until someone answered.

"Room service. What can I help you with, Mr. Johnson?"

He winced at the unfortunate last name he'd used as their alias. "Condoms. I need a box of condoms. Right away."

Silence met his request.

Carol started giggling.

He frowned at her. "There's a hundred-dollar tip if you get them up here in the next two minutes."

"Yes, sir," the clerk said, suddenly sounding eager. "Right away, sir."

Luke hung up the phone. "Johnson. I had to name myself Johnson, then call room service for condoms."

Carol howled with laughter and fell back against the pillows. Luke followed her down, punishing her by tickling her ribs. He followed his hands with his mouth, nibbling and sucking his way across her skin until he settled right where he wanted to be.

She stilled beneath him, her body tensing. "Luke? What are you—"

He fastened his mouth on her.

She gasped and bucked beneath him.

He raised his head. "Do you want me to stop?"

"Don't you dare," she ordered rather forcefully.

He laughed and focused on the delicious task at hand, delighting in the way she moaned and writhed beneath his careful attentions. He was forced to stop when room service knocked on the door. He cursed and grabbed his gun and shoved his shoes on to protect his feet from the broken glass at the door.

"Hurry," Carol panted.

It nearly killed him to leave her for the few seconds it took to throw the money out the door and grab the box from the startled-looking attendant. Luke shoved the door closed, locked it and propped the chair under the knob. Then he ran to the bedroom, shucking his shoes, jeans and underwear as he went.

He dived onto the bed, making Carol laugh at his eagerness. But her laughter quickly turned to sexy mewls of pleasure when he used everything in his arsenal to make her feel beautiful, sexy, cherished. He couldn't make up for five years of hell, but he could take her to heaven for one night.

And that was exactly what he did.

When they were both sleepy and sated and wrapped in each other's arms, she pressed a soft kiss against the side of his neck and settled against him.

"You're an incredible man, Luke," she mumbled, sounding half-asleep. "And not just because you're an amazing lover. You're incredible because I can trust you. You're honest and keep your promises, and I know I can count on you never to hurt me in any way." She kissed him again and was softly snoring a few seconds later.

The warm glow that had filled him after their thoroughly satisfying lovemaking began to fade as her words filtered through his mind. Moments ago he was picturing the two of them after the case was over—going to movies together, taking trips to the mountains, doing everything happy couples did. But now he wasn't sure a happy future was possible. As her bodyguard, he'd made a decision back at the mansion, a decision he'd felt he had to make to try to figure out the identity of the person who was trying to hurt her. It was his primary duty to protect her, so by giving the video card to Alex, that was what he was doing—protecting her.

But as her lover, he knew she wouldn't see his decision as his duty. She would see it as him lying to her, as a betrayal. He'd told her he never broke his promises, and that had always been his policy. But this one time, he'd broken the one promise because she'd be safer if he did.

Now he wondered if he had made a horrible mistake and whether she could ever forgive him for breaking her trust.

## Chapter Thirteen

Carol shook her head as she peered out the living-room window of the hotel suite at the horde of vans and reporters eight floors below in the parking lot.

"I don't understand how they always find me."

"Secrets always end up getting out one way or another, especially where money is to be gained." Luke plopped their bags on the table by the door and double-checked that he'd gotten most of the glass from in front of the door. He couldn't get all the little shards without a vacuum cleaner, but he'd done the best he could. "I think that's everything. Ready to go?"

She dropped the curtain and grabbed the baseball cap Luke had bribed off a passing guest in the hallway. She twisted her thick blond ponytail on top of her head and shoved the cap over it. "I look good, right?" She turned around for his appraisal.

In those tight jeans and that curve-hugging T-shirt she looked so good it hurt, especially since she was smiling and acting so happy this morning, when he knew her happiness would come crashing to a halt as soon as she found out what he'd done.

Maybe he should call Alex and tell him to forget the whole thing. But knowing Alex, he'd probably already started sorting through the video. He wasn't one to put important things aside, especially if it meant possibly catching a killer. Luke should have waited, should have just destroyed the video card in the first place.

"Luke?" Her smile dimmed.

He crossed to her and, unable to resist, swooped in for a quick kiss. She clung to him and was grinning when he pulled back.

"I guess that was a yes," she teased.

His head was still spinning from the kiss. "Yes what?"

She lightly punched him on the arm. "Yes that I look good, of course."

He crossed his arms. "You look way too good, actually. And since we sneaked into the hotel with you in jeans, whoever told the press you were here is probably on the lookout for you in jeans again." He glanced around the suite, then hurried to their bags. He dug in his and pulled out the lightweight jacket he'd packed in case it rained. "This might help disguise those curves a bit. Hopefully that and the cap will be enough to let us make it outside."

She shrugged into the jacket. "Are we going out front again?"

"We're going out a side entrance, either through a delivery area or the kitchens, depending on which one has fewer people around. We'll have to hoof it from there for a few blocks."

"Then what do we do? Walk around Savannah all day?"

"No. I called Trudy while you were getting dressed. She's going to meet us in another rental car."

"Trudy?"

He cleared his throat, not relishing the idea of telling her a former prostitute was running his business while he was gone. "She's my, um, office manager. She's filling in because of…Mitch."

Her smile faded. "I'm sorry."

"I know." He put the luggage straps over his shoulders, as usual keeping his hands free. Then he peered out the peephole to make sure it was clear.

His cell phone vibrated in his pocket. "Just a second." He grabbed the phone. When he saw who was calling, he said, "I'll just be a minute."

She gave him a quizzical look as he headed into the bedroom and closed the door. "Luke here," he said into the phone.

Alex tossed a few choice curse words at him.

"Nice," Luke said. "I didn't even know you knew those kinds of words."

"I want to claw my eyes out to unsee everything I saw on that video you gave me. There were months of surveillance on that card because it only recorded when someone came into the room. You do realize what was on that card, don't you?"

"Yes, unfortunately, I do. I saw a little of it."

"Well, I saw it *all*. It was horrible. Richard Ashton deserved to die."

"You won't get any arguments from me on that. Please tell me you found something that might help with the investigation."

"All right. Your hunch was correct. I found something."

GETTING OUT OF the hotel undetected was easier than Luke had expected. They'd gone through the kitchen and no one had tried to stop them. Just a few startled looks from the cooks, and he and Carol were racing out the side door.

Trudy had been their biggest problem. Luke had given

her the keys to the Camaro in the parking garage so she could drive it back to the office, while he'd taken the keys from her to the Mustang GT she'd rented for them. If Trudy had been Mitch, she would have made the trade and hurried on her way, letting Luke take his client and get her out of danger.

But Trudy wasn't Mitch, and Carol wasn't a typical client. She'd refused to get into the car until she sat on the curb and let Trudy talk to her about how much she missed Mitch and a host of other complaints. It had nearly killed Luke not to grab Carol's arm and haul her to the car. But regardless of his good intentions to keep her safe, he couldn't stomach trying to boss her around or force her to do something she didn't want to do.

Finally, Trudy headed back to the hotel and Carol got into the Mustang. Luke drove through the historic district, keeping an eye on his mirrors, doubling back several times until he was convinced no one was following them. Then he drove into another parking garage. When he turned off the engine and twisted in his seat to face her, Carol was watching him with wary eyes.

"Why are we here?" she asked.

"We need to talk."

"That sounds ominous." She offered him an uncertain smile.

He held his hand out, palm up. As had become her habit, she didn't hesitate. She entwined her fingers with his and they held hands on top of the console between their seats.

"Carol, I need you to keep an open mind. I need you to listen to everything I say before you make any judgments or decisions. Can you do that for me?"

"Okay, now you're scaring me. Just tell me whatever it is that you need to say."

"I need your promise first, to listen until I'm finished explaining everything. You're going to be mad, hurt, but I need you to keep a clear head. Don't jump out of the car or do anything that would put you in more danger."

She bit her lip, her eyes widening. "If this is the 'let's be friends' speech, spare me. It was just one night. It's not like we made a commitment or anything."

In spite of her flippant words, he heard the pain in her voice. He cursed. "I can see I'm making a mess of this and I haven't even started. What I need to tell you has nothing to do with last night, which was completely amazing and wonderful, by the way."

Her hand tightened on his. "Okay. If it's not about… us…then I don't see how it can be that bad. Go ahead."

The way she'd said "us" had him silently cursing in his mind. Carol was special. Whatever fledgling relationship they'd begun to build was too new, too delicate to survive what he was about to tell her. But he couldn't keep her waiting any longer. Waiting, wondering what he was going to tell her, was even more cruel than what he was about to say.

"I gave the video card to Alex Buchanan."

She froze, as still as a deer staring at the rifle that was about to end its life, unable to move or do anything to protect itself. And damn it if Luke wasn't the hunter pulling the trigger.

"I'm sorry, Carol. I know you wanted me to destroy it, but it was evidence. I was worried we might ruin our one chance of finding out who had been in the house, who'd broken into the safe. If they were on the video then we'd have a suspect. Cornell doesn't seem to have any decent leads. Alex's investigator hasn't found anything useful. Every hour that passes makes it less likely we'll catch the killer and more likely your life is in even greater danger. I gave it to Alex so he could—"

"You promised," she whispered. She jerked her hand from his and scooted across the seat until her back was against the passenger door. "You promised me. You said you never, ever break your promises."

He dug his fingers into the console to keep from reaching for her. "And I never do, except this once. Listen to me. I asked Alex to look for evidence, something that would give us a lead so we could tell Cornell—"

Her gaze whipped back to his. "Cornell? You gave him the video card, too?"

"What? No. No, no, no. Alex still has it. I'm not giving it to Cornell unless you give me permission. That's what I need to talk to you about. Alex saw—"

"Everything," she finished for him. "He saw my shame, my humiliation. Did he tell you all the sickening details, Luke?" Tears streamed down her face. "Did he?"

He shook his head. "Carol, listen to me. I need to explain."

"Did he tell you how Richard taught me lessons whenever I displeased him? And how he beat me and raped me over and over? Did he tell you Richard made me apologize to him for the imagined wrongs I'd done, and how he made me tell him over and over again that I loved him, when all I wanted to do was scream at him and tell him how much I loathed and despised him? Did Alex tell you that? Did he?"

His arms ached with the need to pull her to him, to hold her and protect her from the memories and the hurts she'd suffered. He wanted to wipe the tears away and erase the hurt, accusing look on her face, but he knew she wouldn't welcome his touch right now.

Maybe not ever.

"Alex is an extremely private person. He didn't know what was on that card when I gave it to him. I promise you he would never show it to anyone else or even tell them what's on it without your permission."

She laughed harshly. "You promise? Really?" She shook her head. "How do I keep doing this to myself? First Richard, then you. How do I keep attracting the same kind of men?"

Luke stiffened. His chest tightened and for the space of a few heartbeats he could barely breathe. "You're comparing me to the man who beat and raped you? The man who ruptured your spleen and almost killed you?" he rasped.

She opened her mouth several times as if to say something, but then she turned and looked out the passenger window.

Luke stared through the windshield, wondering how he'd become her enemy when all he'd ever wanted to do was to protect her. They were both silent for several minutes, then he started up the car.

"You have a choice to make," he said.

"And what's that?" she asked without turning to look at him.

"Alex saw someone on that video card. They went into the master bedroom and opened the wall safe. They took out a stack of papers. From what he could see on the video, Alex believes you may be right, that the papers were a will. That person knew or at least suspected your husband had another will. And when they found it, they took it so no one else would ever see it. There's a good chance they might be the killer."

She slowly turned and looked at him. "What's this choice that I have to make?"

"Whether or not to give the video to Detective Cornell as evidence."

She shook her head. "No. Absolutely not."

"Without the video, we have no way of pointing Cornell to the person Alex saw, no way of pointing him toward another suspect."

"We have to find another way." She swiped at the wet tracks on her cheeks. "Who's in the video?"

"Leslie Harrison."

She gasped. "No, it can't be. It doesn't even make sense. She was his lawyer. She would have a copy of any will he had, so why care about the one in his safe?"

"Because she didn't want anyone else to see that copy. Because it was a will she had no intention of ever filing. If she filed a fake will, then she had to destroy any copies of the true will before someone found them. And there's something else to consider, something Alex mentioned on the phone. Someone had to tell Richard about the cottage you rented. Leslie is the only person besides you who knew about the cottage."

Carol pressed her hand to her throat. "Oh my God."

"We need to give the video to Cornell."

She shook her head. "No. We need to go see Leslie. I want to give her a chance to explain. If she hadn't helped me, if she hadn't given me the strength and encouragement that I needed to escape, I'd have died from that last beating. She was a good friend. My only friend. She deserves a chance to tell her side of whatever is going on here. Let's go talk to her. She should be at her office."

"That's not a good idea. If she's guilty of wrongdoing, even if she's not the actual person who pulled the trigger, she's got everything to lose. When people are cornered with no way out, it makes them dangerous. We need to call Cornell and let him handle it while I take you someplace away from all this once and for all and we wait there until the investigation is over."

"She's a friend, or at least she was until I turned away from her. I want to talk to her."

Her anger at him was clouding her judgment. Somehow he had to get through to her. He was about to try again when his cell phone buzzed in the holster at his hip. He frowned when he saw the number on the screen but quickly answered.

"Detective Cornell, what can I do for you?"

His hand tightened around the phone as he listened. "Okay. Yes, I'll tell her. Thank you."

He ended the call and put the phone away.

"Tell me what?" Carol asked.

He scrubbed his face with his hands before answering. "I'm so sorry. There's no easy way to say this. Leslie Harrison is dead."

## Chapter Fourteen

"You don't have to do this." Luke paused in front of the Mustang and put his hand on Carol's arm to stop her from going inside the law offices of Wiley & Harrison. "We can wait until Cornell gets all the papers cataloged and back at the station to look at them."

She glanced down at his hand on her arm and arched her brow.

He sighed and dropped his hand.

Without a word, she went with Cornell into the law office.

Luke didn't bother to follow. The place was buzzing with cops, so she was safe, and Carol didn't want him with her anyway. He leaned back against the Mustang and stretched his legs out in front of him to wait.

"Aren't you supposed to be guarding someone?" Alex stepped around the end of the car and leaned back against it beside him.

"I'm not her favorite person right now. She hasn't fired me yet, but it's probably only a matter of time."

"The video card?"

"Congratulations. You're a genius."

Alex laughed and handed an envelope to him, the same one Luke had left for him hidden in the car yesterday.

Luke shoved it in his shirt pocket.

"You do realize that video card ate up the last of any favors I'd be inclined to do for you, right?" Alex said.

"Yeah, I figured. Guess I should have warned you. But I was afraid you wouldn't do it if I told you."

"You tricked me."

"Yeah. I did. But only because I trust you. I knew if you were the one to review the video, nothing would leak to the press or the internet. That would destroy Carol."

Alex was silent for a moment, then he gave him a crisp nod. Apparently Luke was forgiven.

"Speaking of your client, why is she inside? Isn't that where they found Leslie Harrison?"

"The coroner already removed the body. There are papers all over her office that have to do with Ashton Enterprises, so Cornell asked Carol to take a look and see if she saw anything unusual. My turn to ask you a question. What are you doing here? And how did you even know about Leslie's murder? It only happened a couple of hours ago."

Alex smiled in greeting to a couple of police officers he knew as the cops walked around the Mustang and headed inside the building. "Cornell called me. He gave me a briefing of what happened and asked me to meet him here so we could discuss my client."

"Carol?"

"No. Grant."

Luke waited, but Alex didn't seem inclined to say anything else. "Come on. What gives?"

Alex sighed. "Grant posted bail this morning."

Luke's gaze flicked to the law office. "What *time* did he post bail?"

"Three hours ago."

"That's what Cornell wants to talk to you about. He thinks Grant killed Leslie."

"I'm sure that's how Cornell sees it. Grant did go on and on complaining about his brother's will, accusing the lawyer of filing the wrong one. That's public record, by the way, not a client confidence. Grant screamed about the will back at the police station to anyone who would listen."

Luke swore. "He's obviously the killer."

"Innocent until proven guilty."

"You really believe Grant's innocent?"

Alex's lips compressed into a hard line but he didn't answer.

"Screw this." Luke shoved away from the car.

"What are you doing?"

"Getting *our* client out of here before *your* client figures out where she is and tries to kill her, too."

LUKE GLARED AT the police officer blocking his way into the lobby of Wiley & Harrison. "I'm telling you, I'm a bodyguard and my client is inside. I need to see her."

"And I'm telling you, sir, that this is a crime scene and no one goes inside without a badge."

Luke's fingers twitched at his side. He had to remind himself that getting arrested wouldn't help Carol. He resisted the urge to shove the scrawny cop out of his way, just barely.

"You need to leave, sir. You're blocking the doorway."

Luke ignored him and looked over the top of the cop's head. Cornell stood with a group of officers around a young, distraught-looking woman who was dabbing at her eyes with a tissue.

"Cornell," Luke called out. "Call off your Chihuahua and let me inside."

The detective glanced over and rolled his eyes. "Let him in." He waved Luke forward.

The officer grudgingly stepped out of Luke's way.

Luke made a straight line toward Cornell, glancing around the room as he did so, but there was no sign of Carol.

"What's so important you had to bust in here?" Cornell demanded when Luke stopped beside him.

"You didn't tell me Grant Ashton was out of jail when you called this morning."

"I didn't *know* he was out of jail when I called. I found that out on the way here. You might as well wait outside until Mrs. Ashton is finished inventorying the office. There's nothing you can do in here."

"Where is she?"

Cornell jerked his hand over his shoulder. "The middle door on that back wall, Leslie Harrison's office. If you have to go inside, go, but don't touch anything. You know the drill."

Luke frowned. "Why is the door shut?"

Cornell turned around. His brows drew down. "It wasn't shut earlier. Maybe we were too noisy out here for her."

They both headed toward the door.

Luke grabbed the knob, but it didn't turn. "Why is the door locked?" He banged on the wood. "Carol, open the door. It's Luke."

Cornell motioned at the group of police officers he'd just left. "Get the admin to give me the key to the—"

Luke rammed his body against the door. The doorjamb splintered and the door crashed open against the far wall.

Cornell cursed and followed Luke into the room.

Papers were scattered all over the desk and the floor.

But there was no sign of Carol. Luke ran to the only exit, the window behind the desk. He tried to open it, but it was sealed shut. Layers of paint around the frame acted like glue.

"She must have come back out and I didn't notice," Cornell said. He headed into the lobby.

Luke saw an open door on one side of the office. He ran in there. A bathroom, empty, no window, just a skylight, at least twelve feet up.

He ran back into the office just as Cornell rushed inside.

"No one saw her come out of this room," he said. "And the officer at the door to the lobby said she didn't come out that way, either."

Luke continued his search of the room. He felt along the exterior wall, beside the window.

"I'll lock down the parking lot," Cornell said. "I'll get every officer to search the building and all the cars."

Luke stood back and kicked one of the panels in the wall. It flew open, a hidden door, swinging back on hinges to bounce against the exterior wall of the building. Sunshine flooded into the room.

A sick feeling settled in the pit of Luke's stomach. "Too late. She's already gone."

CAROL TWISTED AGAINST her restraints in the backseat of the patrol car, straining her neck to look behind her as the car swung out onto the highway.

She caught a glimpse of the back of the building. Luke's tall, muscular form filled the doorway where she'd been taken just minutes earlier. Carol would have cried out, but her mouth was covered with duct tape. Instead, she renewed her struggles, bouncing on the backseat, trying to get Luke to notice her. But without her hands free to wave, she couldn't do much.

*I'm right here, Luke. Look at me. I'm right here.*

But he didn't glance her way, and the building disappeared as the car careened around a curve.

She strained against the tape around her wrists, thankful they were at least in front of her and not behind her.

Her brother-in-law glanced in the rearview mirror. "You might as well settle down and stop trying to get the tape off. You're just going to hurt yourself."

She put every ounce of contempt and loathing she could into her expression as she looked at him through the wire partition that separated them.

He sighed heavily. "I'm sorry, Caroline. I didn't want to do this."

He wiped a bead of sweat from his forehead and made another turn. They were heading out of town on a two-lane rural road. Where were they? She should have been paying more attention to his driving instead of wasting her efforts glaring at him.

The trees seemed to fly by as they headed deeper and deeper into the woods. They hadn't passed any houses in the past few minutes. He was taking her somewhere isolated. She'd never come down this road before. She was certain of it. A sense of panic started gathering inside her.

Her nose twitched. The smell of…manure…seeped into the car. Were they near a farm? Another smell, thick and heavy, made her gag. The unfamiliar, rancid odor was cloying and sickeningly sweet. What *was* that?

The trees fell away and they emerged from the forest. A line of concrete buildings squatted in the middle of a field a few hundred yards in front of them. There weren't any other cars. No signs of any people around, probably because it was late and anyone who worked here would have already gone home for the day. Up ahead, hanging on the side of the first building, a wooden sign announced the building's purpose. Carol's insides went cold as she read the words: Matheson's Beef Packing Plant.

## Chapter Fifteen

Every detective in the Chatham County P.D. had been called in to brainstorm where Grant may have taken Carol. They were assuming Grant was the culprit, but it wasn't much of a stretch. Beat cops canvassed the area near the Wiley & Harrison law office, but still there were no concrete clues about what had happened.

The conference room was practically busting at the seams, with every seat around the center table taken and officers lining the walls. Luke didn't care that he blocked the view of the shorter men around him. He crowded up to the table so he could hear what Cornell said and see the video playing on the laptop.

"Okay, people, everybody be quiet so we can hear the audio," Cornell ordered. "The part we're most interested in should be coming up soon."

The view was from a security camera in the alley behind the law office. It was black-and-white, grainy, poor quality. Apparently, the law firm had the camera for an insurance discount, but they'd gotten the cheapest equipment money could buy, just enough to satisfy the requirements of their policy. And it showed. The picture wasn't even in focus, but it was better than nothing. Or, at least, Luke sure hoped so. If they could at least get a picture of the car, and if all the stars aligned, a license plate, the police could put out a BOLO to tell every law-enforcement agency in a hundred-mile radius to be on the lookout for the car that had taken Carol away.

They already theorized a car had approached from the woods behind the building, as evidenced by crushed grass, broken branches and tire tracks the techs were examining. But other than seeing that the road led to the highway, they had nothing. And gaining any useful data from the crude tire tracks would take time—time they didn't have.

The seconds ticked by in the lower-right-hand corner of the screen. Something metallic flashed in the trees behind the building. A car drove out of the trees, the metal rack on its front grille mowing down small saplings and making a road where there hadn't been one before.

"I'll be damned," Cornell said. "It's a police car. One of ours." He snapped his fingers. "Quick, someone look up the numbers on the side. Tell me whose car that is."

The car parked behind the building.

"It belongs to Officer Jennings," one of the detectives called out.

"Where is he?" Cornell demanded.

"Vacation. He's been out of town for over a week. He took his personal car. The perp must have stolen his patrol car out of his driveway."

The car door opened on the video and a tall figure stepped out, wearing a ski mask—a very familiar ski mask.

"He's tall, over six foot," Cornell said. "And he's got some muscle to him. That's Grant Ashton."

"We can't be sure without seeing his face." Luke leaned in close to the screen. He shook his head. "It could be Grant or his brother, Daniel. They both have the same build." He straightened in disgust. "It could be anyone."

Cornell flashed him an irritated glance. "How many men do you know that size?"

"Including me?"

Cornell rolled his eyes and studied the screen again.

"He has a key," Luke said. "That's why there weren't any scratches on the lock. He's someone who knew Leslie Harrison, or at least someone at the law office."

The rest of the video went by quickly. It only took Grant, or perhaps Daniel, less than a minute to rush inside and come out with Carol. Her mouth was covered with duct tape and her hands were bound in more of the shiny silver tape. Her abductor shoved her into the backseat of the patrol car, then took off into the same woods from where he'd just emerged.

Moments later, the car appeared off in the corner of the camera's view, coming out of the trees a hundred yards away and turning onto the blacktop highway. In the center of the camera, the door to the building flew open again, and Luke stood in the entrance, looking around.

He cursed as every eye looked at him. He'd been standing there like a fool, looking at the trees and the back of the building. But he hadn't noticed the patrol car driving away with Carol bouncing in the backseat, obviously trying to get his attention.

Cornell stopped the video. "We've got a car and a direction, and a rough description of the doer." He pointed at one of the detectives. "Put a BOLO out and send some uniforms to Officer Jennings's place. See if he's got a security system that might have caught this guy on camera when he stole the car. If not, let's hope he has some nosy neighbors who saw something. And get Jennings on the phone. See if he saw anyone hanging around his place before he went on vacation."

The detective hurried out of the room.

Cornell glanced around the table. "Now, quickly, let's go down the list and see if something pops. What do we have on the Richard Ashton murder?" He pointed at the detective directly across from him. "You, run it down for us."

The detective flipped through the electronic tablet on the table in front of him. "Two gunshots, fired close-range, about five feet away. Bullet was .45-caliber. The only fingerprints at the scene were from the vic, the landlord, the vic's wife and Luke Dawson. The vic's wife and Dawson's prints were limited to the front door. Their alibis checked out."

Luke crossed his arms. "Get on with it," he urged.

"Grant Ashton owns a .45, but it was allegedly stolen last month. He filled out a police report."

"Convenient," Cornell grumbled.

"Gas receipt at a nearby station traced to Grant Ashton," the detective continued. "Surveillance footage showed him gassing up his SUV right around the estimated time of death. He's our prime suspect."

"Put the footage up on the laptop," Luke ordered.

The detective next to Cornell looked to him for permission.

"Do it."

Soon the video was playing and everyone was trying to crowd around the table to see it. The quality was much better than the earlier video. The license plate was clearly visible. No question that it was Grant's car. But the SUV was parked on the far side of the pump and the driver was only a vague image on the camera.

Cornell squinted at the screen. "Could be Grant Ashton. The size fits."

"It could also be his brother," Luke offered. "Or me.

All you know from that video is that someone drove Grant Ashton's SUV to that station and filled the tank. Period."

"All right, what's your theory, then? We're just reviewing the evidence here. If you've got something to add, by all means, jump in." Cornell leaned back in his chair and crossed his arms.

"I don't know why Ashton was killed, or Mitch, or the lawyer. And I don't know why Carol was abducted. All I know for sure is that I can link all those people together with only two other people—Grant and Daniel Ashton. They were Richard's brothers. They both attended the funeral where Mitch was killed. They both knew Leslie Harrison through their brother. And we all know the link with Carol—they're her brothers-in-law. It just makes sense one of them is behind all this. What I want to know is what you're doing to find *both* of them."

One of the detectives across from Cornell spoke up. "Every available beat cop is out looking for Grant Ashton, canvassing everywhere he would go. No one has seen him anywhere."

"What about his house, his family?"

"They're not home. Left yesterday to get away from the reporters that have been hounding them since Grant's arrest."

"What about the other brother, Daniel?" Luke asked.

Cornell looked to his left. "You were in charge of that this morning. What have you got?"

The detective shook his head. "He's not our guy. He's been at work since seven this morning. He's still there, with plenty of witnesses. He's the CEO of his own company. He's been in meetings this whole time. He couldn't have abducted Mrs. Ashton."

"Then we focus on Grant," Luke said. "He's a wealthy guy, just like the rest of his family. What properties does he own? Is there anything like a warehouse or abandoned building somewhere he might take her?"

Cornell frowned. "We're not exactly amateurs here. We've been checking that out since the abduction. No dice so far."

Luke raked his hand through his hair. Carol had been gone for over two hours. What was happening to her? He couldn't even let himself think the worst—that it was already too late. No, she was strong. She'd proved how strong she was by surviving living with her abusive husband for so long. She couldn't have survived that hell only to die now.

He'd promised to protect her. He'd already broken one promise. He wasn't about to break another. He *had* to find her.

"What about Stellar Security?" Luke asked.

Cornell's brows rose. "What about them?"

"They're a common thread. They're linked with everything the Ashtons do. I had an investigator look into them, but he didn't find anything."

"What did you expect him to find? You think one of the security guards is behind the murders and Mrs. Ashton's abduction?"

"No, I think Grant abducted her. But he may have had help. As amazing as Stellar Security is supposed to be, Grant was able to break into the mansion and attack Mrs. Ashton a few nights ago even though they were supposedly guarding the place. And in all the time Mrs. Ashton lived in the mansion, and Stellar Security was there, it seems rather odd they never realized the abuse that was going on. They turned a blind eye to it."

"You think they turned a blind eye to murder, too?"

Luke clenched his fists. "I don't know. I don't have

anything to go on except a gut feeling. Carol didn't trust them. That's why she hired me."

"Looks like she bet on the wrong pony in that race."

Luke didn't bother to glare in the direction of the detective who'd issued that statement in a loud stage whisper. How could he be mad when the detective was telling the truth? Maybe his distrust of Stellar Security was influenced too much by Carol's own fears instead of facts. Maybe if he'd told her to stick with the much larger security firm, she'd be okay instead of out there suffering at the hands of another Ashton man.

He shoved his way through the crowd and opened the door.

"What are you going to do, Dawson?" Cornell called out.

Luke shook his head. For the first time in his career, he had no clue what to do.

LUKE SPENT THE next few hours driving his car every place he knew of that the Ashton family owned—from Carol's mansion in town, to Grant's and Daniel's houses, and even out to the country house where he and Carol had been a few days ago. So far, no luck spotting anything that even hinted that Carol might have been there recently.

He made dozens of calls to everyone he knew in law enforcement. He called the private investigator that Alex had hired and spoke to him about what had happened. He asked the investigator to focus again on Stellar Security, because the more he thought about it, the more their bumbling incompetence seemed glaring, as if it had been on purpose.

When he was at the police station earlier, he couldn't very well have told Cornell that Stellar Security hadn't noticed Leslie Harrison going upstairs and getting into Richard Ashton's safe. He couldn't do that without mentioning the video card, and he certainly wasn't going to do that again.

He winced.

*Please, God, don't let me breaking a promise and betraying Carol be the last memory she has of me.*

A call to a friend at the courthouse landed him an email with a list of every piece of property the Ashtons owned. The list was extensive, over ten pages, and half of the places were within driving distance of Savannah. He forwarded the list to Cornell.

Somehow, there had to be a better way to narrow down where to look for Carol.

He called Cornell and checked in with him frequently, but even though the detective was doing everything Luke would have done in his place, the results were still that the sun was about to set and Carol was nowhere to be found.

A visit to Grant Ashton's house yielded nothing but an aggravated butler who had already been grilled by Cornell's detectives. He emphatically told Luke he didn't know where any of the Ashtons were and the next time someone asked him he was going to fill out a harassment complaint.

Luke drove around with no particular destination in mind anymore. He wasn't surprised when he again ended up outside the office building that Daniel Ashton owned and where he was working today. There weren't that many cars still in the lot since it was so late. Finding Ashton's car wasn't difficult. But even if the lot had been full, he'd know which car was Daniel's. Luke had cashed in just about every favor anyone owed him today trying to get as much information about the Ashtons as he could find. As a result, he knew exactly which car in the parking lot was Daniel's—the forest-green BMW sedan.

Surprisingly, he didn't park in a reserved spot with his name on it as Luke had expected. Instead, he parked way out at the end, near the street. Why? So he could get away quickly if he needed to?

Luke scrubbed his face and rested his head against his seat. He would search every place on the list of Ashton holdings if he had to, but without a starting point, something to help him narrow the list down, it was like looking for the proverbial needle in a haystack. It would take days, maybe weeks, to thoroughly search all those possible hiding places.

Carol didn't have days. She sure as hell didn't have weeks.

He checked his gun at his hip and his backup in an ankle holster. If he thought going into Ashton's building right now and holding a gun to his head would yield any useful information, he wouldn't hesitate. But Cornell's men had already questioned him earlier, and Daniel had been coldly polite, insisting he knew nothing. Luke's hope was that if he followed the man he'd lead Luke to Carol.

Two men emerged from the exit at the back of the building. Luke straightened in his seat. Daniel Ashton was easy to pick out. He towered over the much shorter man walking beside him. The other man talked with his hands as he apparently said something funny. Daniel laughed and shook his head, then waved as the man headed to his car on the opposite side of the lot.

Daniel continued to his car and got in without glancing toward Luke, who was parked in the shadow of some oak trees on the street. Luke waited until Daniel turned the corner. Then he floored the gas and headed after him.

CAROL STUMBLED AND fell onto the hard concrete floor. The door slammed shut behind her before she could make it to her feet.

"Grant," she called out. "Please, don't do this! Let me out of here."

The sound of his footsteps rapidly walking away was his only response.

She ran to the door and tried the knob, unsurprised to find it locked. The upper part of the door was glass, but on top of the glass were iron bars. No way out, unless she could figure out how to pick the lock. That was one "lesson" Richard had never taught her.

She made a quick circuit of the room. A row of tiny windows near the top of the ceiling were too high for her to reach. A fluorescent light illuminated the small room, which wasn't much bigger than her master-bedroom closet at the mansion. The walls were concrete. And there was nothing inside the room, not even a chair to sit in. She moved back to the door. If she was going to get out of here, it would have to be through the door. Somehow she had to figure out a way to get it open.

Would Grant really hurt her? She'd thought so, at first. He'd certainly been rough as he yanked her out of the car and shoved her in front of him, forcing her to go into the processing plant. But he'd turned solicitous, taking her to the restroom and waiting outside for her. Then he'd taken her to an office where he had sandwiches and drinks waiting in a cooler. They'd both eaten in tense silence. She tried to glance around, looking for a way to escape without seeming obvious. He checked the time on his cell phone every few minutes.

They sat in the little office for hours. Every one of her attempts at conversation had been met with stony silence. He'd become more and more agitated the later it got, and when the last of the sunlight disappeared from the windows and he was forced to turn on some lights, he swore and grabbed her arm. He tugged her after him and gave her another chance to use the restroom. She took advantage of every minute he gave her, testing the windows, looking for something she could use as a weapon. He must have grown suspicious at how long it was taking her, because he came in as she was trying to pull a paper-towel dispenser off the wall.

His eyes had narrowed dangerously and, without a word, he'd brought her to this room and threw her inside.

Footsteps sounded again down the hall. She peered into the gloom. A moment later, Grant appeared, carrying what looked like little pieces of paper in one hand and a roll of duct tape in the other.

She moved back from the door, rubbing her wrists at the memory of the tape he'd wrapped around them earlier. But he didn't open the door. Instead, he ripped a piece of tape off the roll and used it to hold the pieces of paper in place on the glass part of the door.

When he was done, he tossed the roll down and motioned her forward.

She hesitated, then moved to the door. She glanced at the papers and realized they were computer printouts of pictures. She gasped and pressed her hand to her mouth when she realized who was in the pictures—Grant's wife and daughter. They were both tied up, blindfolded, gagged. Carol couldn't even tell if they were alive or dead.

Her gaze flew to Grant's.

"I didn't kill Richard, or that photographer." His voice sounded muted through the thick glass. "But I did kill Leslie, and I'll kill you, too, if I have to." He tapped the glass above the pictures. "Daniel took them, Caroline.

And if I don't do what he wants, he'll kill them." He tapped the glass again. "I would do anything for them, Caroline. Anything. Even if that means slaughtering you like one of the cows they butcher in this place."

He turned on his heel and disappeared down the hallway.

Carol sank to the floor and covered her face with her hands.

## *Chapter Sixteen*

Daniel Ashton didn't seem to be in a hurry to get home. Then again, he didn't have anyone waiting for him. He was single, never married, no girlfriends or even close friends that Alex's investigator had been able to find. The P.I. had called while Luke tailed Daniel through the city. The only real news he'd been able to tell Luke was that he'd traced Stellar Security through dozens of holding companies to its real owner.

Daniel Ashton.

Luke had immediately called Cornell and told him the news. He also reminded Cornell that Mitch had once worked for Stellar Security and had quit to work for Luke. While Mitch had never shared the details of why he'd quit, Luke knew something ugly had happened while he'd worked there.

Luke would lay odds that the "something ugly" had to do with Daniel Ashton, either directly or indirectly. And now Mitch was dead. Luke had had a crash course today during all those phone calls about the Ashton brothers, and it wasn't a pretty picture his contacts had painted.

The brothers had always been rivals, but with Richard and Daniel in particular, that rivalry went to extremes. Carol was the one who'd told Luke that Daniel didn't visit the mansion much anymore. And while Luke didn't have proof yet, he'd heard speculation that the reason for that was because Richard and Daniel had gone after the same acquisition, a business takeover, and Richard had come out the winner.

Daniel had never forgiven him.

The business Richard bought had taken him from millionaire to billionaire in less than a year. But Daniel was still a mere millionaire and appeared to blame his brother. The only question was, did he blame his brother enough to kill him over it? Or had the other brother held a grudge no one knew about and *he* was the one who'd decided to shoot Richard?

At this point, Luke didn't care which one had killed Richard. They were both dangerous, a pit of vipers. But they were still family, and Luke was betting Carol's life that there was a bond between the two brothers, a bond that meant that Daniel knew where Grant was.

DANIEL SMILED AT the waitress and stood to leave the restaurant Luke had tailed him to half an hour earlier.

Luke held a menu up in front of him. As soon as Daniel went outside, Luke would scramble after him again and see where else the man went.

"Mr. Dawson, fancy seeing you here."

Luke slowly lowered his menu.

Daniel Ashton stood beside the table, staring down at him as if he were the worst kind of vermin, his mouth curling in contempt. "Why are you following me?"

Luke tossed the menu on the table and slid out of the booth. He rose to his full height, which was only an inch taller than Ashton, but it was enough to make Daniel's smug look fade. He seemed to assess the breadth of Luke's shoulders as they stood toe to toe.

"Where is she?" Luke asked.

Daniel arched a brow. "'She'? I'm sure I don't know who you're talking about."

Luke grabbed Ashton's lapels and slammed him against the nearest wall.

Diners at the next table gasped in shock. Excited voices rose from the nearby waiters.

Luke ignored all of them and pressed his hand against Daniel's throat. "Tell me where she is, you filthy piece of—"

"Now, now," Daniel clucked. "No reason to act so uncivilized, Mr. Dawson."

"Sir, you need to let him go before we call the police."

Luke glanced over his shoulder. A group of five men stood behind him. Three appeared to be waiters. The others, judging by their clothing, were the bartender and the restaurant manager.

"You heard the man, Dawson. Let me go. Now."

The laughter in Ashton's voice had Luke gritting his teeth. He forced his hands to relax their death grip on the other man's lapels and he took a step back.

Daniel straightened his collar, frowning at the wrinkles Luke had made. He flicked the fabric and gave Luke a smile that didn't come close to reaching his cold, dead eyes.

"You should try the filet mignon in this restaurant, Mr. Dawson," he said. "I hear the meat's never frozen. It's freshly butchered." He laughed as if at a private joke and headed out the front door.

Luke moved to follow, but the restaurant manager stepped in front of him. "Hold it, sir. I think you should sit and calm down. Whatever happened between you two—"

Luke shoved the man out of his way and ran through the double doors to the street.

The sound of squealing tires had him turning to see

Ashton's green BMW speeding away. Daniel lifted a hand
out the window, waving, before the car turned down a
side street and disappeared.

Luke cursed viciously and ran to his car. But ten minutes later he pulled to the curb and slammed his fist
against the dash. No sign of Daniel Ashton. His last link
to the man who'd taken Carol was gone.

Or was it?

He stilled, thinking about the list of holdings on his
phone and the last words Daniel had thrown at him.

*You really should try the filet mignon. It's freshly
butchered.*

He fumbled for his phone and opened the email. He
quickly scrolled through the list. Yes, there, on the fifth
page—*Matheson's Beef Packing Plant.* Sweat broke out
on his brow.

*Oh, God. Please. Don't let her die like that.*

He slammed his foot on the accelerator and rocketed
away from the curb, praying harder than he'd ever prayed
in his life that he wouldn't be too late.

CAROL SHIVERED IN the concrete room. It might have been
hot outside, but the air-conditioning in the plant kept it
chilly, and the longer she was there the colder she became. As minutes ticked away and Grant didn't return,
she began to wonder if it wouldn't be better to just try to
go to sleep and hope she was cold enough to succumb to
hypothermia. It had to be a better way to die than whatever her brother-in-law had planned for her.

She closed her eyes and leaned her head on her arms,
resting on top of her drawn-up knees. Footsteps sounded
outside the room, but not just one set. This time, there
were two. She jerked her head up. Grant rounded the corner, and beside him was Daniel.

The chill that went through her had nothing to do with the temperature in the room.

The men stopped at the door.

"Open it," Daniel ordered.

"Not until you tell me where you're holding Susan and Patty. That was the deal."

Daniel calmly raised his hand and shot Grant in the forehead. He dropped to the floor like a rock.

Carol screamed.

Daniel pointed the gun at her through the glass. "Shut up."

She clamped her shaking hands over her mouth.

He took out a handkerchief and wiped the specks of his brother's blood off his face. He put the handkerchief in his suit pocket then unlocked and opened the door. "Hello, there, dear sister-in-law. It's been a while, if we don't count that little visit at the hospital, or the exchange of pleasantries at the funeral. Before that, I hadn't seen you in a year or more, I suppose."

He clucked his tongue and shook his head as he stepped into the room. "Not my choice, I assure you. Entirely your late husband's. Tell me—" he crouched down in front of her and used his gun to tilt her chin up "—did you miss me? No? I missed you very much. You see, I've always wanted you." He slid the cold barrel of the gun down the side of her neck, then across her lower lip. "Grant wasn't the only person who argued with Richard. He and I argued, too, about business and money mostly. But that wasn't *all* we argued about."

He slid the gun lower, until it pressed against the valley between her breasts.

Carol flinched and flattened herself against the wall behind her.

He smiled, as if delighted by her reaction. "Richard

caught me sneaking into your room when you'd gone to bed early one night. I'd told him I wasn't feeling well and wanted to lie down in the guest room for a bit before driving back home. I guess he didn't trust me, so he checked on me at a most inopportune moment." He laughed. "I wanted you. And he wouldn't let me have you. And that's the *real* reason he died." He grimaced. "Unfortunately, dear old Grant over there suspected I was up to no good. It's a long story, really, and I don't have the time. Suffice it to say, I have contacts in security, and I knew exactly where you went every time you left the house. I knew Leslie was helping you." He shook his head. "She paid for that, of course, after doing me a favor or two. Like switching wills."

"I...don't understand." She tried to keep calm, to keep him talking, stalling for time. "Why would you switch wills? You didn't get much money in the will Leslie filed."

He shook his head. "Still haven't figured it out, have you? I didn't want all that money going to Grant. I wanted it for myself. I knew the courts would suspect something if I got the bulk of the estate, so I played it the other way. I would have gotten all the money eventually, of course. When I married you."

She shivered with revulsion.

His smile faded. "Richard would have knocked you flat for that." His eyes flashed with anger. "I'd planned on killing him at that little cottage of yours and framing Grant. You know, two birds, one stone. But 'Grant the pest' followed me, walked right in after I shot Richard. From then on, it was all about damage control. I'd hoped to make Grant look like a lunatic, a three-way lovers' triangle. I was having fun framing him for everything I was doing, but things got so screwed up."

Nausea coiled in her stomach. She pointed at the pictures on the glass door. "What about Grant's family? They never did anything to you."

"True. Their fate is regrettable, I agree. They were nice enough to me. But they're collateral damage. Nothing anyone can do for them now."

Carol looked past him to the open doorway.

His brows rose. "Thinking you can get by me, eh?" He stood and pulled her to her feet. He reached a hand toward her face.

She flinched and ducked away.

His nostrils flared like a stallion scenting a mare. "Skittish, huh? Well, I can understand that, after living with my brother for so long. I never was one to hit a woman. Not that I have anything against the practice. It just wasn't my thing." His gaze raked down her body. "As for the rest, well, like I said, if I only had the time." He clucked his tongue again and shook his head. "What a waste."

He stepped back and motioned with the gun toward the door. "Come along, Caroline. The only way I'm coming out of this without going to prison now is to make sure no one can connect me to anything. That's why I had Grant kill Leslie and abduct you. I needed him to leave evidence that showed he was a psychopath and a murderer. When you both disappear, the police will assume he killed you and ran off. And I can go back to my life as if nothing ever happened." He waved the gun again. "Let's go. The plant opens in a few hours. I have to get rid of both of your bodies and hose the place down before anyone sees me. Time to disappear."

Carol lunged past him and ran out the door into the hall.

The sound of laughter followed her mad dash through

the plant. There weren't that many lights on, only an occasional overhead round fluorescent light hanging from a pole that didn't illuminate much of the area around it.

"I'll just get rid of Grant first, okay, Caroline?" he called out. "Don't worry, it won't take long."

A whimper bubbled up in Carol's throat. Why wasn't he worried she'd escape? She soon found the answer. When she reached the door she and Grant had come through earlier, it was bolted shut with a chain and a padlock across it. She shoved on the door anyway, rattling the chain and rocking the door against its frame.

Daniel's laughter echoed through the room. "That's the only door, sweetheart," he yelled from somewhere in the darkness. "The only other way into the plant is through the cattle shoots. And they're all closed up nice and tight for the night."

Carol whirled around, her gaze sweeping back and forth across the low, rectangular building. The room was full of all kinds of equipment she didn't recognize, scary-looking machines with sharp blades and what looked like giant nail guns hanging from pulleys on the ceiling with rubber hoses attached to them. She turned in a circle, but it looked as if Daniel was telling the truth. The only other doors were the massive overhead rolling kind, like garage doors, only they were closed and she didn't have a clue how to open them.

The sound of footsteps against the concrete floor had her crouching down behind the nearest machine. Another sound followed in concert with the footsteps, a swishing sound, like fabric brushing against something. She leaned around the machine, peering across the dimly lit area where the sound was coming from.

Daniel passed beneath one of the lights, calmly walking through the warehouse, holding Grant's hand, dragging his body behind him.

Carol clasped her hands over her mouth again, desperately trying not to wretch.

Laughter sounded from the other side of the room again. Daniel must have heard her, and he was enjoying her terror.

An image of Luke's handsome, smiling face floated in Carol's mind's eye. If he were here, he'd protect her. He'd make everything safe for her. For a moment, she remained frozen wishing Luke could save her. But she thought about the pictures on the glass door in the room where she'd been held. Grant's wife and daughter didn't deserve to die any more than Carol did, assuming they were still alive. If she gave up now, she wasn't just letting herself down. She was letting those innocents down, as well. She couldn't cower and do nothing. She had to at least try to escape and get help for them.

She forced her shaking legs to carry her forward, into the dark, to try to find another way out or a weapon of some sort. She stumbled over a hose and fell against a smooth concrete wall in the middle of the room. She leaned over it, peering down into the darkness, following the wall as it snaked back and forth on itself through the room.

It was a cattle shoot, one of the serpentine enclosures the cows walked through from the stockyard to where they were slaughtered. She glanced at the heavy doors behind her. They didn't sink into the floor. They rested flat against the concrete. But the cattle shoots were below floor level, like a subway. Maybe Daniel was wrong. Maybe there *was* another way out. Maybe there were side rooms off the shoot or a control panel that would raise the doors.

She glanced around but didn't see him anywhere. She braced her hands on the smooth top of the wall, lifted her legs over the side, then dropped down into the darkness below.

# Chapter Seventeen

There was no sign of movement near the main building of the meatpacking plant. Luke sprinted from the wooded area where he'd parked and quickly crossed the short distance to the parking lot. He crouched beside the patrol car Grant had stolen and felt the hood. Cold. He hurried to Daniel's BMW and knelt down behind the rear bumper, watching the building.

"Their cars are both here," he whispered into his cell phone. "And there are lights on inside the main building, the one with the stockyards out front. Don't come in hot. You'll have to come in without sirens or lights. I don't want you to spook them. Have you contacted the plant manager to bring the keys?"

"He'll meet us a quarter mile outside the entrance. Just keep the line open and let us know if you see anyone outside," Cornell said. "ETA about fifteen minutes. Do not engage the suspects."

"To hell with that, Cornell. If Carol's inside, there's no telling what could be going on. I'm not waiting."

"Just a minute, Dawson. You can't just—"

Luke punched the button to end the call, then turned the ringer off. He shoved the phone into the holder on his belt and pulled out his pistol. As a force of habit, he popped the clip and double-checked the loading, then popped it back in. He waited a few more seconds, closely watching the high-up windows for movement and observing the shadows around the building.

A distant whining noise filtered from inside the building. Luke's stomach dropped. He knew that sound. *An electric saw.* He took off running toward the entrance.

CAROL DUCKED DOWN at the loud noise. It was coming from another part of the building—close…too close. She swallowed against the thickness in her throat, shying away from admitting to herself that she was pretty sure what that sound was. And since it seemed to be coming from the direction where Daniel had dragged Grant's body, she had a good idea what was going on.

She closed her eyes and pressed her hand to her mouth, trying not to gag. The sound stopped. Her eyes flew open. She had to get moving, had to find a way out. Now.

She took off running down the constantly winding shoot again. It was dark, but since the top was open, the dim light in the factory filtered down enough for her to see where she was going. The walls smelled of disinfectant with an occasional waft of manure. She tried breathing through her mouth and forced herself to keep going even though the shoot never seemed to end.

The tunnel came to an abrupt stop at a solid metal door. She slid to a halt, feeling the door, but there was no knob. She pushed against it, but it didn't budge. A bitter curse word flew through her mind. She was trapped. And all Daniel had to do was peer over the top of the concrete walls and follow them to the end. Then he could aim his gun and shoot her as if she was nothing more than a helpless cow waiting to be slaughtered.

"Oh, Caroline," Daniel's singsong voice called out. "Where are you, dear?"

He was so close! Had he heard her pressing on the gate? Was he about to peer over the wall at her? She bit her bottom lip and started forward, trying not to make any sound that would give away her location while she headed back the way she'd come.

"What are you doing down there, Caroline?"

She gasped and looked up. Daniel was casually leaning over the sloped top of the wall directly above her, shaking his head. "Do you know why the shoot curves back on itself so much instead of going in a straight line? Cows, when they get scared or confused, like to turn around and go back where they came from. So, even though we build the tunnel too narrow to allow them to turn around, we curve the tunnel back on itself. It fools the animals into thinking they're going back where they came from, when really they're getting closer and closer to the end, where death awaits. The animals stay calm the entire time." He grinned. "Makes the kill easier. Brilliant, don't you think?"

Carol whimpered and started running.

"There you go. That's a good girl. Run all the way to the end. You're just making this easy."

She stumbled to a halt and glanced uncertainly behind her.

"Now, now. We can't have you turning around." He leaned over the wall above her and aimed his gun. She screamed and took off running. The gunshot echoed through the tunnel behind her.

THE SOUND OF a gunshot froze Luke on the platform outside the window. He hadn't been able to get inside through the main door because it was chained. The only other possibility seemed to be one of the windows set high up in the wall. He'd used the access stairs for the roof to get to one of the windows. He used the butt of his gun like a hammer and busted the glass. He yanked off his leather jacket and flipped it over the jagged edges in the frame and climbed through the hole, then dropped to the floor.

He landed in a rolling crouch to break the long fall, then leaped to his feet waving his gun in front of him. He hurried out the door, pausing when he saw a trail of blood across the concrete. As if a body had been dragged through the hall.

*Please don't let it be Carol.*

He rushed out the door into the darkness beyond.

CAROL STOPPED AND flattened herself against the wall. What was that sound? Breaking glass? She looked up. Daniel must have heard it, too, because he'd paused and looked back toward the front of the building. He looked down at her and smiled, then pressed his fingers to his lips as if to tell her to be quiet, before disappearing over the edge of the wall.

Were the police here? Or Luke? She waited, hoping to hear sirens or voices, but all she heard was silence.

"Hello?" she called out. "Is someone there? It's Carol Ashton. Is anyone out there?" She waited. Nothing. Could anyone even hear her down in this pit?

She debated running back toward the gate, but that was a dead end, a trap. The only way out was up ahead, where the cattle were slaughtered. Bile rose in her throat but she fought it down and took off running again.

A MUFFLED SOUND echoed from somewhere up ahead. Luke peered into the gloom and listened intently. Another sound, like someone…running? He spotted curving concrete walls in the middle of the room. They ended at the beginning of the assembly line, where heavy drill-looking machines hung from the ceiling—probably the pneumatic guns used to kill the cattle before they were processed.

The sound echoed again. It was definitely coming from that concrete opening. He glanced around, then sprinted to the nearest curve in the wall. He looked over the side and caught a glimpse of someone running.

Relief swept through him.

"Carol," he called out in a low whisper.

She stopped and jerked her head up, her eyes wide. "Luke, watch out!"

He whirled around and kicked in one movement, catching Daniel Ashton in the chest. Ashton grunted and fell against the concrete wall. The gun he'd been holding went skidding across the floor and wedged up beneath a machine.

Luke brought his own gun up, but Daniel lunged at him before he could get off a shot. His arms wrapped around Luke, forcing his gun hand up. They both tumbled to the concrete floor.

Daniel landed on top of Luke and bit down on Luke's wrist. Luke shouted and tried to shake him, but his hand went numb and the gun dropped from his fingers. Daniel grinned triumphantly and dived for the gun. Luke flung himself on top of Daniel's leg and yanked back, pulling him across the floor before he reached the gun.

Daniel cursed and twisted beneath him, sending a punch flying at Luke's jaw. Luke ducked just in time, but his movement allowed Daniel to scurry out from beneath him and lunge to his feet. The gun was a few feet behind Luke now, but he couldn't grab it without taking his eyes off Daniel.

His foe seemed to weigh the choices in front of him,

glancing from the gun to Luke and back again. His mouth twisted in a bitter smile. He lunged toward the gun, but when Luke moved to intercept him, Daniel whirled around and sprinted into the darkness, disappearing behind a row of machines.

Luke grabbed the gun and ran to the concrete wall. He peered down but didn't see Carol anywhere. He looked back up, keeping an eye out for Daniel, then raced along the curve of the wall, glancing down every few feet, looking for Carol.

He ran all the way to the end of the tunnel before he found her, standing in the slaughter box, her eyes wide, her body shaking as she stared at the bloodstains on the floor beneath her.

"Carol," he whispered. "It's Luke."

She didn't respond. She kept staring at the blood, her face alarmingly pale.

Luke glanced around. "Sweetheart, listen to me. It's Luke. Can you tell me where Grant is?"

She finally looked up at him. "Grant?" She shook her head. "Grant is…Grant is…" She closed her eyes and swallowed.

He knew the end of that sentence. Grant was dead. Luke couldn't say that bothered him a bit. It meant one less lunatic to deal with before Carol was safe.

He peered into the gloom. There was a light directly over the slaughter box, which made it difficult to see anything else, like someone shining a flashlight in his eyes.

"I have to go find Daniel. Wait here."

She shook her head back and forth. "No, no, don't leave me! Don't leave me here!"

His heart broke at the terror on her face, in her voice. "Okay, okay. First, take my gun. Just in case. Here, take it." He tossed it down to her.

She caught it and looked at it as if she didn't have a clue what to do with it.

Luke gritted his teeth. He glanced around one more time, the hairs standing up on the back of his neck.

"Luke, please, help me." Carol reached her arms up toward him.

He flattened himself on the floor at the edge of the box and hung down over the opening, his arms outstretched. "Take my hands. I'll pull you up."

She shoved the gun into her waistband and raised her hands.

A swishing noise was Luke's only warning. He dived to the side just as Daniel lunged at him with one of the pneumatic drills hanging over the slaughter box. It fired, the steel bolt slamming against the concrete before retracting, ready for another shot.

Carol screamed from below.

Daniel bellowed his rage and whirled around, knocking Luke flat on his back. Daniel slammed the drill down toward Luke. Luke clasped his hands on the sides of the drill, grappling for control.

Noises sounded from the front part of the building, voices yelling, feet shuffling. A loud pop echoed through the room. One of the rolling doors began rising.

Daniel cursed and renewed his struggles. The drill lowered closer, closer. He smiled, smelling victory. Luke bucked and twisted beneath him. Daniel lost his grasp on the drill and fell to the side. He must have seen the gun holstered on Luke's ankle because he cried out in triumph and yanked the gun out. Luke grabbed the drill and twisted around just as Daniel came up with the gun.

Luke shoved the drill against Daniel's head and squeezed the trigger.

A sickening crack echoed through the room. Daniel's eyes rolled up in his head and he fell to the floor. He didn't get back up.

"That was for Carol and Mitch, you piece of filth," Luke rasped.

"Police! Freeze!" someone yelled behind him.

Ignoring the order, he tossed the drill aside and crawled the last few feet to the slaughter box. The sound of running feet echoed behind him. He reached down and pulled Carol up and out of the box. Her eyes widened as she looked past him at Daniel's body lying on the floor. Her fingers dug into his shirt. He twisted to block her view, cradled her in his lap and pressed her face against his chest.

She sobbed and a flood of tears soaked his shirt.

"It's okay," he whispered against her hair. "It's okay. It's over. You're safe. You're finally safe."

## Chapter Eighteen

*Three months later*

Luke leaned his forearms on his new desk and looked through the glass wall of his office into the main room of Dawson's Personal Security Services. Fifteen other shiny new desks sat in the enlarged space. He'd rented the office next to his and had knocked down the wall in between to expand. He'd hired eight more bodyguards and an admin assistant to help Trudy since her workload as office manager had gotten so heavy.

The notoriety from the Ashton case had gained him more paying clients—*well*-paying clients—than he could handle. And it didn't hurt that Stellar Security had suffered a severe blow after the investigation proved Daniel Ashton had been fed information from GPS locators on his family's vehicles and that some of the guards had even spied for him. They'd looked the other way when asked—like the night Grant Ashton allegedly "broke into" the mansion.

Business was good, but it didn't bring the joy or sense of accomplishment he'd hoped for. Nothing these days did. And he knew why.

*Carol.*

He hadn't seen or heard from her since that harrowing night at the packing plant. They'd both been brought into separate interview rooms at the police station where they'd each given their statements about everything that had happened.

Cornell had sent his men to all the Ashton warehouses in the city to search for Grant Ashton's family, based on the warehouse in the background of the pictures Grant had taped to the door at the plant. His hunch had paid off and Grant's wife and daughter were found safe. It had taken a few hours, and Luke had stayed in Cornell's office receiving minute-by-minute updates, until it was over. Then he'd gone out to update Carol, but she was gone.

Luke pulled his top desk drawer open and unfolded the single sheet of paper she'd asked Cornell to give him that night.

*Luke, I'm sorry to leave things this way, but I have to get out of here. I'm leaving Savannah and all the ugliness behind. I don't know if I'll be back. Thank you for being there for me. You kept your promise. You saved me. That's a debt I can never repay. All I can say is thank you, and goodbye.*

He refolded the note and dropped it back into the drawer. Blowing out a deep breath, he shoved his chair back and crossed to the window to stare down at the street below.

Behind him, in the outer office, the little bell Trudy had insisted on putting above the door tinkled, announcing they had a visitor. Luke didn't bother to turn around. Trudy had taken her role of replacing Mitch as office manager quite seriously. She was like a little general, bossing the bodyguards around, undaunted by the fact that most of them were well over a foot taller than her. Luke had yet to see anyone Trudy couldn't handle.

"Well, hello, there," Trudy called out, obviously recognizing whoever had come in. "It's good to see you again. What can we do for you today?"

"I need a bodyguard."

Luke froze at the sound of that soft, achingly familiar voice. *It can't be.* He slowly turned around.

Carol stood fifteen feet away, her startlingly blue eyes meeting his, her pink lips curving into a smile. "Hello, Luke."

Trudy glanced back and forth between them, then— for once—melted quietly away to the far side of the room without saying a word.

Luke stepped out of his office and stopped in front of Carol, his hungry gaze drinking her in. "You colored your hair brown."

She patted her hair as if self-conscious. "It's as close to my natural color as the stylist could make it, for now, until the roots grow out."

"I like it."

"Thank you."

He wanted to reach for her, to pull her against him. Instead, he shoved his hands in his pockets and cleared his throat. "You told Trudy you needed a bodyguard. Someone's bothering you?"

"No. No one's bothering me."

He frowned. "But you need a bodyguard?"

"Well, I suppose to be more accurate, I'd have to say I need *the* bodyguard. The bodyguard who saved my life a few months ago." She stepped forward, until the toes of her heels pressed against the toes of his dress shoes. "I need *you,* Luke."

Afraid to hope, he cleared his throat again. "You might

need to spell this out for me because I have a feeling I'm misunderstanding you. After that night at the plant, you left. You didn't wait to talk to me. You didn't answer my calls or letters. That doesn't sound like you need me."

She glanced around the office, at the handful of bodyguards trying to pretend not to listen to them. Trudy didn't even bother pretending. She sat at her desk, her head in her hands, unabashedly staring.

"Is there somewhere…private…where we can talk?"

He stepped back and waved her toward his office. When she stepped inside, he closed the blinds on the glass walls and door, then turned to face her. "All right. No one's watching, or listening. Except me."

She bit her bottom lip and crossed the room to stand in front of him again. She held her hand out. "Hi, my name is Carol Bagwell. I legally changed my last name. I'm an Ashton no more."

He shook her hand and smiled reluctantly. "Believe me, you were never an Ashton. You've always been better than that."

She grinned. "I think so, too." Her grin faded. "Luke, when I left Savannah, it wasn't you I was leaving. It was…everything that had happened. I was confused, scared. I needed to get my head on straight. I went from living with my controlling, critical parents to living with a husband and having my every action, my every thought, controlled by him. When you came into my life, you were too good to be true. But I wasn't ready for you. I didn't even know who I was anymore. I needed time, and space, to figure that out."

"Where did you go when you left?"

"As far away as I could get without leaving the country. I went to the West Coast, to Seattle. But I couldn't escape my past by running away. I had to work with lawyers to settle the Ashton estate. They located Richard's true will at Wiley & Harrison and refiled. Grant's wife and daughter got nearly half the estate. The other half went to Daniel. True to his nature, Richard left me nothing." Her lips curved in a smile. "But Daniel didn't have a will, and no spouse or children. So the court awarded Daniel's portion to me. I hope Richard is turning over in his grave right now."

Luke smiled. "Good for you."

"I gave it away, though," she said.

He coughed. "What?"

"The money. Half a billion dollars in assets. I gave it to a women's charity. They're going to build a halfway house for abused women right here in Savannah. And with all that money, they'll be able to help women all over the country. Isn't that wonderful?"

He ran his finger down her soft cheek. "I think you're the most kind and generous woman I've ever met. Personally, I'd have kept a few million. But I understand why you didn't want to keep your husband's money. You wanted a fresh start. Right?"

"You *do* understand. I knew you would. I'm in therapy, probably will be for a long time. I'm a mess, actually, in a lot of ways. But I'm growing stronger every day. And there's one thing for sure that I know that I want."

"And what's that?"

"You. I want you. That is, if *you* still want *me* now that I'm a pauper."

He spanned her waist with his hands and set her on the desk so they were almost at eye level. "Carol," he said, "I'm in love with you, in case you haven't figured that out."

He covered her lips with his and consumed her in a searing kiss. Her arms wrapped around his neck, pulling him tightly against her as she kissed him back. When they broke apart, they were both out of breath.

He leaned down and kissed the side of her neck.

She shivered. "Luke?"

"Hmm?" He kissed her collarbone.

"When I told you I gave away a half a billion dollars, I may have neglected to mention something."

He moved to her ear and sucked her earlobe between his teeth.

She gasped. "Luke!"

He laughed and pulled back, looping his arms around her waist. "I don't care how poor you are, or what kind of trouble or baggage you bring with you. I'll take you any way I can get you." He leaned in for another kiss, but she pressed her hands against his chest, stopping him.

"I just need to make sure there's complete honesty between us."

He grimaced. "The video card, right? I destroyed it. I got it back from Alex and I cut the thing into pieces. Then I burned it. I'm so sorry I broke my promise."

She blinked. "The video card? No, no. That's ancient history. I understand why you felt you had to do that. I'm the one with a secret this time." She chewed her bottom lip. "I did give away half a billion dollars, but my portion of the estate was a little bit more than that. I may not exactly be a pauper."

"Oh? Exactly how much are you *not* a pauper?"

She grinned. "I might still have a few million dollars left over."

He laughed and swept her into his arms. "At least I'll know you don't like me for my money. I'm not exactly hurting these days, in case you hadn't noticed. Now, if you're through with all this talking, the rest of this… conversation…requires a bit more privacy."

She giggled and looped her arms around his neck again. "Lead the way, bodyguard. Lead the way."

\* \* \* \* \*

## COMING NEXT MONTH FROM

# HARLEQUIN
# INTRIGUE

### Available May 20, 2014

## #1497 RESCUE AT CARDWELL RANCH
*Cardwell Cousins* • by B.J. Daniels
When Texas P.I. Hayes Cardwell arrived for his brother's wedding, he didn't expect to play hero. But after he saved McKenzie Sheldon from abduction, he couldn't get her out of his mind and heart. Can he protect her from a killer hiding in plain sight who's about to spring a final trap?

## #1498 TRACELESS
*Corcoran Team* • by HelenKay Dimon
Corcoran Team leader Connor Bowen is desperate to locate his kidnapped wife, Jana, who walked out on him seven months ago. Can Connor get to her—and reconcile—before time runs out?

## #1499 THE RENEGADE RANCHER
*Texas Family Reckoning* • by Angi Morgan
Nearly broke, Lindsey Cook turns to rancher Brian Sloane for help. But will Brian uncover the motive and unmask the killer before he annihilates the entire Cook family?

## #1500 GROOM UNDER FIRE
*Shotgun Weddings* • by Lisa Childs
When Tanya Chesterfield's groom is kidnapped, she marries her bodyguard so she can meet the terms of her grandfather's will, collect her inheritance and pay the ransom. But there's no ransom demand made— only attempts on her life and her new husband's life.

## #1501 SHATTERED
*The Rescuers* • by Alice Sharpe
It's up to adversaries-turned-lovers Nate Matthews and Sarah Donovan to disrupt a sinister terrorism plot aimed at striking fear in the hearts of every person in the country....

## #1502 THE DEFENDER
by Adrienne Giordano
Sparks fly when sassy Chicago defense attorney Penny Hennings teams up with FBI agent Russ Voight to catch a murderer. But will Penny sacrifice both their lives to get justice? _____

**YOU CAN FIND MORE INFORMATION ON UPCOMING HARLEQUIN® TITLES, FREE EXCERPTS AND MORE AT WWW.HARLEQUIN.COM.**

HICNM0514

# REQUEST YOUR FREE BOOKS!
## 2 FREE NOVELS PLUS 2 FREE GIFTS!

**⬡ HARLEQUIN**

# INTRIGUE®

## BREATHTAKING ROMANTIC SUSPENSE

**YES!** Please send me 2 FREE Harlequin Intrigue® novels and my 2 FREE gifts (gifts are worth about $10). After receiving them, if I don't wish to receive any more books, I can return the shipping statement marked "cancel." If I don't cancel, I will receive 6 brand-new novels every month and be billed just $4.74 per book in the U.S. or $5.24 per book in Canada. That's a savings of at least 14% off the cover price! It's quite a bargain! Shipping and handling is just 50¢ per book in the U.S. and 75¢ per book in Canada.* I understand that accepting the 2 free books and gifts places me under no obligation to buy anything. I can always return a shipment and cancel at any time. Even if I never buy another book, the two free books and gifts are mine to keep forever.

182/382 HDN F42N

Name _____ (PLEASE PRINT) _____

Address _____ Apt. # _____

City _____ State/Prov. _____ Zip/Postal Code _____

Signature (if under 18, a parent or guardian must sign) _____

**Mail to the Harlequin® Reader Service:**
**IN U.S.A.:** P.O. Box 1867, Buffalo, NY 14240-1867
**IN CANADA:** P.O. Box 609, Fort Erie, Ontario L2A 5X3
**Are you a subscriber to Harlequin Intrigue books
and want to receive the larger-print edition?
Call 1-800-873-8635 or visit www.ReaderService.com.**

* Terms and prices subject to change without notice. Prices do not include applicable taxes. Sales tax applicable in N.Y. Canadian residents will be charged applicable taxes. Offer not valid in Quebec. This offer is limited to one order per household. Not valid for current subscribers to Harlequin Intrigue books. All orders subject to credit approval. Credit or debit balances in a customer's account(s) may be offset by any other outstanding balance owed by or to the customer. Please allow 4 to 6 weeks for delivery. Offer available while quantities last.

**Your Privacy**—The Harlequin® Reader Service is committed to protecting your privacy. Our Privacy Policy is available online at www.ReaderService.com or upon request from the Harlequin Reader Service.

We make a portion of our mailing list available to reputable third parties that offer products we believe may interest you. If you prefer that we not exchange your name with third parties, or if you wish to clarify or modify your communication preferences, please visit us at www.ReaderService.com/consumerschoice or write to us at Harlequin Reader Service Preference Service, P.O. Box 9062, Buffalo, NY 14269. Include your complete name and address.

HI13R

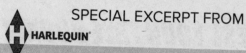
Hayes stepped out into the cool night air and took a deep breath of
Montana. The night was dark, and yet he could still see the outline of
the mountains that surrounded the valley.

Maybe he would drive on up the canyon tonight after all, he thought.
It was such a beautiful June night, and he didn't feel as tired as he had
earlier. He'd eat the sandwich on his way and—

As he started toward his rented SUV parked by itself in the large
lot, he saw a man toss what looked like a bright-colored shoe into his
trunk before struggling to pick up a woman from the pavement between
a large, dark car and a lighter-colored SUV. Both were parked some
distance away from his vehicle in an unlit part of the lot.

Had the woman fallen? Was she hurt?

As the man lifted the woman, Hayes realized that the man was about
to put her into the trunk of the car.

What the hell?

"Hey!" he yelled.

The man turned in surprise. Hayes only got a fleeting impression of
the man, since he was wearing a baseball cap pulled low and his face
was in shadow in the dark part of the lot.

"Hey!" Hayes yelled again as he dropped his groceries. The wine
hit the pavement and exploded, but Hayes paid no attention as he raced
toward the man.

HIEXP69764

The man seemed to panic, stumbling over a bag of groceries on the ground under him. He fell to one knee and dropped the woman again to the pavement. Struggling to his feet, he left the woman where she was and rushed around to the driver's side of the car.

As Hayes sprinted toward the injured woman, the man leaped behind the wheel, started the car and sped off.

Hayes tried to get a license plate, but it was too dark. He rushed to the woman on the ground. She hadn't moved. As he dropped to his knees next to her, the car roared out of the grocery parking lot and disappeared down the highway. He'd only gotten an impression of the make of the vehicle and even less of a description of the man.

As dark as it was, though, he could see that the woman was bleeding from a cut on the side of her face. He felt for a pulse, then dug out his cell phone and called for the police and an ambulance.

Waiting for 911 to answer, he noticed that the woman was missing one of her bright red high-heeled shoes. The operator answered and he quickly gave her the information. As he disconnected he looked down to see that the woman's eyes had opened. A sea of blue-green peered up at him. He felt a small chill ripple through him before he found his voice. "You're going to be all right. You're safe now."

The eyes blinked then closed.

*Can he protect her from a danger that's much closer than they think…a killer hiding in plain sight who's about to spring a final trap?*

*Find out what happens next in*
*RESCUE AT CARDWELL RANCH*
*by* NEW YORK TIMES *bestselling author B.J. Daniels,*
*available June 2014, only from Harlequin® Intrigue®.*

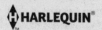

# INTRIGUE

## AN UNDERCOVER AGENT WILL TRAVEL TO THE UNFORGIVING UTAH DESERT TO RESCUE HIS WIFE IN HELENKAY DIMON'S LATEST *CORCORAN TEAM* NOVEL.

Connor Bowen hasn't seen his wife since she left him seven months ago claiming he was more married to his job than he was to her. Now his dangerous past has plunged Jana into mortal danger. This time the former Black Ops agent won't let anything come between him and the woman he'd lay down his life to protect.

Jana moved across the country to start over—far from the haunting memories of Connor. But after she's brutally abducted, she has to once again rely on the take-no-prisoners Corcoran Team leader for survival. Across the desolate, rock-strewn desert, Jana and Connor race to uncover the link to his past before the killers hunting them succeed in their deadly mission.

# TRACELESS
## BY HELENKAY DIMON

*Only from Harlequin® Intrigue®.*
*Available June 2014 wherever books are sold.*

HI69765

# HARLEQUIN®

# I N T R I G U E®

### A TEXAS RANCHER FINDS TROUBLE ON HIS DOORSTEP IN THE FORM OF A KILLER'S BEAUTIFUL TARGET...

It's clear to Texas rancher Brian Sloane that Lindsey Cook will be a serial killer's next victim. For twenty years someone has been systematically killing off her family in "accidents," and recently her car was deliberately run off the road. The handsome cowboy is willing to be the protector the gorgeous blonde wants—but unwilling to act on their instant attraction. Before long, the search for Lindsey's stalker leads Brian into more trouble...and right into Lindsey's arms. After one smoldering kiss, he knows there'll be no turning back. Though never one for relationships, he'll risk his life for her...and the surprising secret her family has been dying for.

# THE RENEGADE RANCHER

## BY ANGI MORGAN

*Only from Harlequin® Intrigue®.*
*Available June 2014 wherever books are sold.*

HI697663

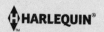

# INTRIGUE®

## I NOW PRONOUNCE YOU...
## BODYGUARD AND WIFE?

When her real groom is kidnapped, Tanya Chesterfield
convinces bodyguard and former flame Cooper Payne to
marry her in order to fulfill the terms of her inheritance
and secure a possible ransom. But when there are no
demands for money, only attempts made on Tanya's life,
Cooper's protective instincts go into overdrive. Nearly
losing her makes Cooper realize he never stopped loving
her, and their pretense as husband and wife resurrects the
passion between them. Cooper has vowed to honor and
cherish her, and he is determined to find the truth—even
if it means in the end he must let Tanya go.

# GROOM UNDER FIRE
## BY LISA CHILDS

*Only from Harlequin® Intrigue®.*
*Available June 2014 wherever books are sold.*